WEIRD HORROR

NO.2

WEIRD HORROR 2
SPRING 2021

© Undertow Publications and
its contributors

PUBLISHER
Undertow Publications
1905 Faylee Crescent, Pickering
ON, L1V 2T3, Canada

Undertowpublications.com
WeirdHorrorMag@gmail.com

EDITOR
Michael Kelly

STORY PROOFREADER
Carolyn Macdonell

LAYOUT
Sam Cowan

OPINION
Simon Strantzas

COMMENTARY
Orrin Grey

BOOKS
Lysette Stevenson

FILMS
Tom Goldstein

COVER ART
Nick Gucker

**COVER AND
MASTHEAD DESIGN**
Vince Haig

INTERIOR ART
Wesley Edwards

WELCOME to issue #2 of **Weird Horror.**

From September 1 through to October 15, 2021, we will be open to submissions of fiction for issue #4. We will open in April 2022 for issue #5.

FICTION GUIDELINES

For issue #4 (March 2022) **Weird Horror** Magazine is open to fiction submissions from September 1 through to October 15. Submissions must be original and previously unpublished anywhere, in any format, on any platform. Please do not query about reprints.

It may take the full submission period to respond. Simultaneous submissions are welcome. Please inform us if your story is accepted elsewhere. No multiple submissions. Please send 1 story.

We are actively seeking new and underrepresented voices. We accept submissions from anyone, regardless of race, gender, or sexuality.

We are seeking pulpy dark fiction in the weird fiction and horror genres of 500 to 6,000 words. **(Please respect our word counts. Query first for longer pieces.)** Monsters, ghosts, creatures, fiends, demons, etc. Dark crime. Suspense. Mutants. Killers. Ghouls. Golems. Witches. Pulpy goodness!

Payment is 1-cent-per-word, with a $25 minimum (paid via PayPal) for first worldwide English-language rights, for use in the print and eBook editions. We ask for a 6-month exclusivity. Copyright remains with the author, and a contract will be provided.

Submit stories in Standard Manuscript Format as a Word document or PDF, and e-mail as an attachment to: *WeirdHorrorMag@gmail.com*

Please format the subject line of your e-mail thusly: Submission - Story Title - Author Name

Please keep your cover letter short.

Submissions sent outside the submission period will not be read.

Please query if you have any questions.

ADVERTISING

Get your unique brand in front of our unique readers!

A full-page ad is just $60 (U.S.) per insertion. A half-page ad is $40. Ad space is very limited. We reserve the right to refuse unsuitable material. Please contact us at WeirdHorrorMag@gmail.com.

Michael Kelly

Strange! Eerie! Uncanny! Macabre!

| Issue 2 | Contents | Spring 2021 |

Welcome to the new pulp! Weird Horror magazine is a venue for fiction, articles, reviews, and commentary. Published twice yearly — Spring and Fall.

OPINION

SIMON STRANTZAS ON HORROR

A Firm Grounding in
the Knowable World

RECENTLY FOUND myself reading the fiction of a well-known, award-winning short story author whose fiction straddles the lines that separate Fantasy from Horror from Science Fiction. One might call it "literary fantasy", but seeing as subgenres are as amorphous as a cloud of mustard gas it's best not to worry about labels. Suffice it to say this author's stories, while incorporating bits of Horror, would not be classified by most as Horror, and that difference helped me solidify some thoughts I hadn't been able to before.

If Science Fiction is inherently about how things might one day be, and Fantasy is about how things might have been different, then Horror is about how things really are. It's a genre that functions best when directly reflecting of our actual living experience, one that uses metaphor to highlight our fears and anxieties so we might work through them. Or, in some cases, wallow in them. It isn't an optimistic genre, but neither is it necessarily pessimistic. It aims instead to be a realistic portrayal of our worlds—both the exterior and the interior—and its explorations are designed to better illuminate those worlds.

Which isn't to say one can't find something immediately meaningful in Fantasy or Science Fiction (the idea that these genres are devoid of this level of introspection is absurd). But in their cases, the introspection is too divorced from the immediate. It's filtered through an alien landscape (whether that be a futuristic world or alternate past), and while for some this abstracted reality may open up a new level of understanding, for me it creates a distance from what the story wants to say.

There are different ways to tell a speculative story. If we take as a given that all stories are about characters to which we can relate (whether positively or negatively), then the only effectual differences among genres are the environments those characters inhabit and the extra-personal forces that act upon them. These are further complicated by aspects like time (which transforms the realism of today to the unrealism of the past) and location (the realism of one culture becomes the strange unrealism of another), but I think the basics of environment-versus-threat remain. As a result we end up with four broad supersets of stories: those set in realistic environments where realistic things happen (as in, for example, a crime thriller); those set in unrealistic environments where unrealistic things happen (as in, for example, a high fantasy); those set in unrealistic environments where realistic things happen (as in, for example, an alternate history); and those set in realistic environments where unrealistic things happen (as in, for example, a horror story).

Every reader will have supersets they prefer, and some readers may appreciate all four, but my interests have always been rooted in ordinary worlds faced with extraordinary threats—or, more commonly in terms of horror fiction: Supernatural Horror. For me, this is the most rewarding speculative genre, even if it's not the most marketable.

Plenty of Fantasy and Science Fiction readers want nothing more than to be transported by a story, to live inside it and spend time with its characters, inside its world. And to keep readers immersed and fulfilled the authors of these often door-stopping volumes are keen to learn the mystical secrets of world-building. I suppose it makes sense: if you're going to write a door-stopper of a book, you need to invest that world with as many details as you can. Give them a crash-course in that fantastical place and its history so when the intrusion happens, the reader has some context for how wrong it is. But you'll notice that, exclud-

ing one or two notable examples, very few authors writing Horror stories today work at similar lengths. There aren't that many door-stopping Horror novels anymore, if there ever were. There are market reasons and financial reasons for this, but I'd also argue horror stories don't need the extra pages. You needn't build a world if the reader already knows it.

It's not that I can't on occasion appreciate fiction set in an alternate world, but I find the further that narrative world deviates from our shared reality the less interesting it is. And, at least in terms of horror, the less successful. To my mind one of the most important pillars of horror is a firm grounding in the knowable world. This is how the genre works best. The reader must innately understand the natural rules of the world to fully experience terror when those rules are broken by the intrusion of a supernatural force, whether it be a ghost, or zombie, or vampire, or werewolf, or double. These thing are other, and their mere existence threatens us because they upset the natural order. When the world of the story doesn't adhere to this order—whether because it's set in a speculative future or alternate past—the reader is prevented from achieving that level of existential fright when confronted with the supernatural. Because what is the supernatural when there is no natural? It's why a troll's appearance in a Fantasy story doesn't evoke the same dissonance it would in a Horror story. There is no disconnect for the character or reader; no frisson generated by a world different from our own. The bond is broken.

In fairness, there are successful examples of horror stories that take place in worlds other than our own. Many of these are hybrid fantasy stories but of those told strictly through a horror lens the most successful seem to be those where the other world and the horrific intrusion are one in the same. The frisson comes from how that world differs from our own, not in spite of it. Take as example the Natural Horror story, where our known world is in fact not so known at all, and we find the natural world, which we once thought was routine and commonplace, is actually something unusual and bizarre—not so much transformed as revealed. It can be startling, and in a supernatural context it may do more than present a good yarn—it may also erode, if only momentarily, the reader's confidence in their own reality. That sort of lingering effect is more fulfilling than the transactional horror traditional other-based intrusions may provide.

But, at the end of it all, perhaps the reason horror works best when set in a recognizable world is because of the one question that underlies all horror stories: could this happen to me? Because, really, how safe are we? Horror would suggest not safe at all. There's something coming for me, for you, and if by chance or by fate we meet it we may not survive. It's this underlying threat that powers Horror, and it's easier to instill when the distance between we readers and the character we're reading is as narrow as possible.

GREY'S GROTESQUERIES

by Orrin Grey

DARK AND DEEP:
DUNGEON CRAWLS AND HOLLOW EARTHS

The ecology of the dungeon is what fascinates us. The endless maze of twisting rooms, each one seemingly isolated from the next—and in that isolation, things grow strange.

Beyond the next door, it is possible to imagine anything: a forest of fungi as tall as trees; a rift of glowing crystals that seem almost to sing a luring song; an archaic torture chamber, the instruments stained with old blood; the caged and malformed experiments of some rogue alchemist, like a zoo from hell.

So drawn are we to the weird potential of these subterranean realms that Dungeons & Dragons—the game that puts them first right in its title—eventually converted them into a whole region in its most famous setting, a sort of world-dungeon, an entire chthonic realm with its own empires and hamlets, highways and byways, flora and fauna.

Even its name—the Underdark—suggests weird connotations. Wasn't it Neil Gaiman who summarized the Lovecraftian cosmic horror worldview as "there are things in the darkness beneath us that wish us harm?"

The distinct dungeon may date back to the origins of games like D&D, but this fascination with worlds within worlds—worlds of gods and monsters beneath our feet—is older even than the many books from which the earliest iterations of the game took their cues.

In his introduction to Universal's 1956 film *The Mole People*, Dr. Frank Baxter—the "gesture professor," as the wags from *Mystery Science Theater 3000* dub him, for his heavy reliance on hand movements—also introduces us to Hollow Earth Theory.

"There's nothing new about this," he tells us. "It's as old as man, this belief that under the surface there may be areas inhabitable by man." He talks of John Cleeves Symmes and Cyrus Teed, of Dante and Gilgamesh.

"Primitive man," he says, "going into caves, reaching back and back and down and down, wondered what lay beyond, and in terror he fled out." Even once this proverbial "primitive man" was back in the relative safety of the sunlit surface, "He remembered strange sighs and noises."

If that doesn't sound like the beginning of a weird tale, I don't know what does. And, indeed, the writers of *Weird Tales*—and lowercase weird tales—frequently introduced elements

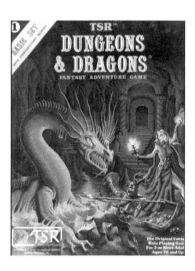

of the Hollow Earth into their stories, sometimes as actual scientific theory, more often for that same potential that can be found in the endless subterrene rooms of a dungeon crawl.

Even Poe dabbled in the subject in his "MS. Found in a Bottle" and his 1838 novel *The Narrative of Arthur Gordon Pym of Nantucket*, which predates Jules Verne's famous stab at the subgenre in 1864's *Journey to the Center of the Earth*—which posits not a Hollow Earth, but simply an enormous cavern large enough to contain a chthonic sea.

Subgenre it was, too. Wikipedia calls it "subterranean fiction" and, besides those notables, lists plenty of other examples, from Edgar Rice Burroughs to Howard Waldrop.

More recently, Rudy Rucker made Edgar Allan Poe himself a protagonist in his 1990 novel *The Hollow Earth* while Scott R. Jones dedicated an entire anthology to the subject in *Chthonic: Weird Tales of the Inner Earth*, in which I have a story, part of a larger "Hollow Earth" cycle that I've been working on.

So, obviously, I've got an interest in the form, and I'm far from alone. Mike Mignola heavily incorporates the lore of the Hollow Earth into his Hellboy mythos, drawing inspiration from places like Edward Bulwer-Lytton's 1871 novel *The Coming Race*, a book with a history as weird as anything Mignola himself could conjure.

Bulwer-Lytton's novel tells of a mystical energy source called "Vril" that will be familiar to anyone who has read much of Mignola's Hellboy oeuvre. When it was first published, several prominent theosophists and occult theorists—including Madame Blavatsky, who makes a notable appearance in Mignola's *other* major comic series, *Baltimore*—believed that the book was based at least partly on "occult truth." Later accounts even suggest that there was a secret "Vril Society" in Weimar-era Berlin.

Even if it isn't true, that sounds like the kind of decadent embellishment that would be right at home in a Hanns Heinz Ewers story—or a Hellboy comic.

As I mentioned, the Hollow Earth plays a big role in the mythology of the Hellboy universe. From it come Hollow Earth people, created as slaves in the distant past, who rose up to overthrow their masters and

The Mole People (1956)

assault the surface world with enormous Art Deco machines. To it ventures Frankenstein's famous creation—in a story that is an obvious nod to Waldrop and Steven Utley's "Black as the Pit, From Pole to Pole"—where he finds a primordial land of dinosaurs and stranded British explorers.

Many of the earliest Hollow Earth stories were Utopian novels, as was the style at the time, and even in Mignola's universe, where Frankenstein's creation initially believes that he has found his way into hell, there is a repeated refrain that, "If there is any future for man, it will be underground." A refrain that finds itself borne out at the end

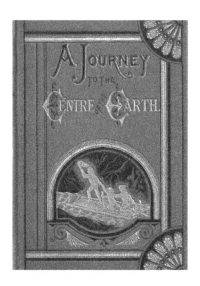

of the saga of Mignola's Hellboy and the Bureau for Paranormal Research and Defense.

Nor have I done more than scratch the surface of all the places—both weird and Weird—that the Hollow Earth shows up. It's there in the recent movie version of *Aquaman*, starring Jason Momoa, and in the popular indie video game *Undertale*.

In Dungeons & Dragons, it is a chthonic world bored full of endless passages and caverns, filled with dark elves and mind flayers; in Burroughs and Hellboy, it is a jungle land of eternal sunlight, populated by dinosaurs and strange beasts; in the recent *Godzilla: King of the Monsters*, it is the cradle of an ancient, kaiju-worshipping civilization, filled with portals that the eponymous giant uses to traverse the world quickly.

Whatever form it takes, from darkest dungeons to sunlit jungles, the idea of a world going on underground remains fascinating for its seemingly endless potential. And not a distant potential, separated from us by gulfs of space, but one that could be just on the other side of the next door...

FICTION

UNMASKINGS

by Marc Joan

Christman watches.

Underfoot, grass stiffens in February's chill; ahead, dusk paints the lake's waters dark as a pike's eye.

They have lit the torches now: balls of fire atop metal stakes. These, smoking and blazing every twenty feet, mark the way from the house to the water's edge. Each stake bears a blue ribbon tied in an extravagant bow. The wind tugs at them as if to steal these pretty things; they flap and curtsy in the flames' radiance. In the folly, too, something burns; light jumps in its windows. But the yew maze is a tunnelled nest of shadows.

Christman walks.

The guests chirrup and cluster like lovebirds displaying bright flightless wings, but their costumes mean nothing to Christman. *Beneath the masks, all are mutton.* Satin and chiffon; organza and lace; ruffed collars and jewelled gloves: all will peel, as easy as skin.

Here is play, says Christman. *Here is sport.*

There, a tall man. His robes are black, his smiling mask is black; black his crown, and black horns adorn it. But his cape is of peacock feathers; it wraps him all about with a watchful iridescence. There, two women; their matching gowns are embroidered with tiny mirrors, so that they glint and shimmer as they walk. Black veils, strung with pearls, hang from their elaborate head-dresses. Beneath the veils, their white, doll's-face masks wait, as unreadable as the dead. They are like twins.

Christman watches. *Oh, my pretty ones.* They glide towards the folly.

Christman follows. *Perhaps. Perhaps.*

ᢙᧄᧄ ᧄᧄᢙ

"Think of it as an experiment," said Aebersold. He came from Graubünden canton, and his French, though fluent, staggered under its Swiss-German burden. "Our little experiment." He placed the pile of masks in front of him, face down, on the table. He patted the pile, very gently, and then put his hands on the table, one to each side of the pile. He grinned at his audience; a silver tooth glinted in the day's last light.

There were four of them at the table, listening to Aebersold: Isobel and three others. Before today, Isobel had met none of her three neighbours; indeed, she'd hardly met Aebersold. She'd corresponded with him in the preceding months, of course, by email and phone, but had seen him face-to-face only once: during last week's psychological tests. Presumably it was the same with the others. She glanced at them. Like Isobel, the woman was in her late twenties. The two men were older, but still the younger side of middle age. Just a few of the many who'd answered Aebersold's advertisement in the *Tribune de Genève.*

And now they, the chosen few, sat around a polished rosewood table in Aebersold's enormous office—a room almost as large as Isobel's entire apartment—in his mansion just outside Geneva. All listening to the strange man who had recruited them for ... for what? A *little experiment.*

ᢙᧄᧄ ᧄᧄᢙ

Christman walks. *My pretty ones.*

Wait. There: a group dressed like Christman. Grey, hooded robes, unembroidered, bare of pattern, as simple as cassocks. One of the group is a child. The child carries a small Swiss flag, red as a berry, tied to a stick. They all wear identical masks; rigid face-coverings, white as an altar cloth. Masks chosen for the poor.

The group moves on. Christman walks alongside. Not so close as to invite speech; not so far as to make speech inaudible. The child is talking.

Christman listens.

ᢙᧄᧄ ᧄᧄᢙ

"This is, deliberately, the first time we have convened as a group, so allow me, if you please, to summarise what I have covered with each of you individually."

Aebersold gestured towards the French windows. His audience of four turned and looked through the glass panes. Close-mown slopes of fine grass fell away to Lac Leman's dull waters. On the left, halfway to the lake, the tall yew hedge was broken by an arched opening; the maze's entrance. The hedge's long shadow marked the day's end. Further off, on the right, giant cedars stood in a cluster; between their trunks, glimpses of white hinted at the folly's pale walls. There, refreshments waited in front of a huge fireplace. Isobel knew all this from the tour Aebersold had given them, less than an hour ago. The estate had been empty then, but no longer. Increasing numbers of people were wandering here and there in ones or twos, or gathering in small groups. But such people; such clothes; such visions of fantasy!

"As you know, tonight is the night of my Masquerade. I have hosted this event each February since moving here ten years ago. The Masquerade's reputation now, I believe, at least among the cognoscenti, surpasses that of Venice's Carnival. Anything Italy can do, Switzerland can do better, eh? Look at Ticino!" Aebersold grinned again. Isobel looked at his hands, lying on the rosewood like two hairless, eyeless creatures taken from a deep cave. She remembered the primitive strength of his grip when they'd shaken hands.

"Such success can largely be attributed to the nature of my guests, who, naturally, come from my own social circle. Individuals with key roles in business or government or medicine. Progressive thinkers, highly-placed in our Universities or international institutions." Aebersold widened his eyes as if in amazement at the elevated company he kept. "Some share my own passion for the study of human psychology; some do not. But all have this in common—they have sufficient wealth and taste to acquire truly remarkable costumes. You see, if my Masquerade is to remain outstanding, and I intend it to do so, my guests *must* be outstandingly attired."

Aebersold's guests followed his nodded glance again; just outside the French windows, two people hesitated at the threshold. One was dressed as a Pierrot, but a Pierrot from fever's dreams: his chequered costume was strung with brightly painted animal bones, and black tears coursed down one cheek. His companion, her face made up as a skull, her hair covered by a black velvet top-hat, wore a shoulder-to-ankle coat of crimson suede. The Pierrot raised a gloved hand in apology, and they turned to walk away.

༺ ๑ ๑ ༻

"But *why* do we need to keep the masks on, Maman?"

"That's what the rules say, darling. That's what the gentleman wants us to do."

"It's uncomfortable. I don't like it."

"But we're having *fun*, darling. And it costs us nothing, for the whole evening. Let's go and watch the performers, by the lake. Do you remember the acrobats we saw last year?"

"No. Why isn't Auntie Beatrice here?"

"She's working late. Maybe she'll come later. She'll come and look for you if she does turn up."

"But how will she find me, when we all look the same?"

"There aren't many children your age here, and you'll be the only one with a little flag. Just wave it around every now and then … Eloise, please stop grabbing onto me like that."

"I'm scared of getting lost. I don't know who's under the masks." The child grips harder. "I'm scared."

"Okay—look, I will make it so you can always see where I am." The woman fumbles under her cloak, and then looks around in exasperation. "Ah! Here. I will wear one of these. Then all you need to do is look for somebody wearing a blue sash, like this." She pulls at a ribbon on a nearby torch; waving the smoke away from her eyes, she undoes its bow, and ties the blue band around her upper arm.

༺ ๑ ๑ ༻

"The festival," Aebersold continued, "nevertheless remains egalitarian, in the sense that local residents also may attend, for free. All I ask is that they follow my rules. Namely: they must leave their mobile phones and cameras in their cars, or at home, as must you; and they, like you, must wear the costumes I provide, at all times. Only simple robes and masks, but they suffice. "

I see, thought Isobel. *A Masquerade with two types of guest: Eloi and Morlocks: betas and deltas; rich and poor. And I, I am of the underclass. As usual.*

Aebersold reached down to a box beside his chair. He brought out four shrink-wrapped parcels of clothing, placed them on the table and pushed them across the polished surface. "Here. Take the one that is labelled with your name."

Isobel unfolded her robe, and stood to hold it against herself. It was a dark, dense material, heavy as a horse-blanket; a head-to-ankle hooded cloak. Like a monk's alb, but in dark grey. The hood had four eyelets sewn into its hem, two on each side, as if to allow the wearer to lace up the opening.

"You will see many others wearing identical robes," said Aebersold. "People from the local community, as I said. And over their faces, they will all be wearing these." He showed them a thin, plastic mask: the standard Carnival design, with its merciless, inhuman Carnival smile. He held it to his face and looked at each of them in turn. When he looked at Isobel, she felt as if something were moving over her skin.

༺ ๑ ๑ ༻

Christman lets the grey-robed group pull ahead to the lake's shore. There is entertainment there, by the water: acrobats, fire-breathers, clowns. A Roman centurion juggles with short-swords; blades flash in the light. A black man in an Ali Baba costume walks on his forearms; his back is bent such that his feet rest on his own head. A Harlequin contorts like an ape.

Yes, the poor grey folk will stay awhile to watch all this. Christman has time enough.

When Christman draws level with the group again—never close enough for questions, never out of reach—another torch has lost its blue ribbon.

꧁ ꧂

"*Your* masks, however, are different." Aebersold gestured to the small pile of masks face-down on the table in front of him. He patted this little stack, moved it slightly away from him, and then back again; as if he had decided to push it across to his four listeners, but reconsidered. He paused, playing with a deeply engraved signet ring on one hand. Isobel noticed that his fingers, significantly broader at the knuckle than at the tip, curled naturally towards the palms; the nails were carefully groomed, but longer than most men kept them.

Just like Papa's hands. Isobel touched her wrists, one after the other, as if feeling for bruises.

"Before I give you your masks, let me remind you again of the terms in the contract you have signed. You will wear your mask and robe at all times during the night's masquerade, under all circumstances. You will not remove the mask until you return to my study tonight, or until you are informed that the experiment is over—whichever is the sooner. In either event, you will only remove the mask in this room, under my supervision. In return for your compliance with these conditions, you will receive the fee stipulated in my original advertisement. Clear?" Isobel shrugged; the men grinned and nodded. The other woman said "Perfectly." Aebersold smiled. He looked at Isobel and adjusted the ring on his finger. Up and down, up and down. Isobel, arms folded, held his gaze.

꧁ ꧂

They are watching the entertainment. Harlequin swaggers and sways; he pretends to fall; he writhes, miming a grotesque pain. *No,* thinks Christman, *that is not how agony looks.*

The crowd mills. All is happy confusion. Christman moves closer.

Harlequin tries to trip the contortionist; the

child's mother claps. The centurion threatens Harlequin's neck with a sword; Harlequin runs. The grey-robed group follows. They shout and scream: pantomime encouragement and pantomime abuse. The child drops the flag and squats to retrieve it.

Now, thinks Christman.

꧁ ꧂

One of the men had a question: "We can go anywhere?" he asked. "There are no restrictions?"

"Absolutely! Wherever you like. Just like any other guest. The folly, the gardens, the lakeside walk, the maze. There is a little, ah, circus by the lake. The maze, by the way, is very simple; to reach the centre you simply turn alternately right, then left, at each branch point. First right, then left. But I don't recommend it at this time of day. There is no lighting in there. Okay?"

Meaningless issues, pointless questions, thought Isobel. *People are stupid.* "You were talking about our masks," she said, before the man could respond to Aebersold. "You said there was something different about them."

Aebersold raised his eyebrows and nodded, like a teacher who has discovered a clever student.

"Quite right." He reached inside his jacket pocket and brought out four envelopes. He put these beside the pile of masks. "Your masks are different in that each is a true and fair likeness of a *real individual*. Four different individuals, that is."

He paused again, nodding in his irritating way. "You understand? This evening, you will appear, each of you, as another. The identity of the individual whose face you will assume will be provided to you." He waved the envelopes at them. "But there is a procedure to follow. First you put on the robes. Then I help you with the mask. And then, only then, I explain who you are. Okay?"

They murmured agreement, and, under Aebersold's expectant gaze, pulled the dark cassocks over their heads. The cloth *smelt* clean, thought Isobel, but *felt* dirty. As though someone had sprayed deodorant over a butcher's smock.

꧁ ꧂

"Maman?"

Christman, finger to mask's lips, holds the child's elbow. On Christman's arm, the ribbon dangles its blue hook; the little fish sees. Christman's back is to the group of grey cassocks. The child is hidden by Christman's robes and by the dark, dark night.

The child walks with Christman. Christman cannot tell if its mask and robes cover a boy or a girl.

It does not matter.

Christman moves away from the group, choosing an angle that puts a flaming torch between them and the child's carers. Once beyond the torchlight—and they are rapidly beyond it—Christman and the child are invisible.

Christman grips the child's arm more tightly, and walks more quickly.

"Maman? What are we doing?"

"It is play," says Christman. "It is sport. A game."

Christman's voice is not Maman's voice. The child's face contracts with every child's worst fear. Tears threaten; horror holds them back.

"It is a game," repeats Christman.

⁂

"So, ladies and gentlemen, let us begin! I will, if you please, see each of you individually in the adjacent room. Starting with … "(Aebersold picked up the masks in one hand and looked at the first of the envelopes in his other hand)"… starting with Isobel."

Isobel followed him out of the office, the cassock's hem rubbing at her ankles. They walked a short way along a corridor and into another room. Aebersold shut the door behind them. The drawing room, Isobel guessed. On a side table by one of the settees, a thick candle burned, its flame motionless. Beside it lay a small knife with a round-ended blade, like a butter-knife. Aebersold placed the masks and envelopes beside the knife.

"First of all, your face for the evening. No, *please*—for experimental validity, you must not look at the front of it—just pull the elastic back over your head. And now bring forward the cassock hood: there." Aebersold stood back; through the mask's eyeholes, Isobel saw him looking at her. He was breathing more quickly.

"Good. But remember, it is essential that the mask is not taken off, even by accident. Which is why I must insist that you permit a fastening—do you see?"

Aebersold held up a thin cord, perhaps three or four feet long. It was the same grey as Isobel's cassock and hood. He passed it through the eyelets just behind the hem of the hood, and through corresponding eyelets on the mask's edge; like lacing a boot. Then he passed the ends of the cord around Isobel's neck and back again. Isobel tensed and took half a step back as he pulled a knot tight under her jaw; he was pulling it too hard, raising her chin so that she had to look at him. The cord pressed against the back of her neck; she could not move away. Even through the mask, she could smell his breath.

"Calm yourself, Isobel, please. This is only to ensure that there is no cheating. You understand, I cannot watch all of you at all times. So I need to verify that the masks are not removed. My method is a little medieval …" (holding onto the noose with one hand, he reached down to the table with the other, picked up the knife and used it to dig up some soft wax from the top of the candle with the knife) "… but foolproof. Look, I put some wax on the knot, so, and then I make the impression of my ring, so, and *voila*, as you French say."

The mask was like an itch that could not be reached, an irritation which extended over her entire face. She adjusted its position as far as she could, but it made no difference to a discomfort that she had not anticipated. She was too hot; she found it difficult to breathe; the mask impeded airflow; the noose was too tight about her neck. But she had agreed to do this—and she needed the money. The humiliation of poverty!

"Thank you, Isobel. And now, of course, you will want to know whose likeness you have assumed. So, who are you?" He offered her an envelope with her name on. "Please. Open it."

Isobel took the envelope from him. It wasn't sealed; all she had to do was open the flap and pull out the single sheet of paper it contained. The paper was folded once. She pushed apart the folds and read out the two printed words: HERR GENIPPERTEINGA.

⁂

At the maze's black entrance, Christman pauses. The child whimpers.

"Maman wants me now," says the child.

"I want you more," says Christman.

In the maze, yew walls tower and press. Their dense growth kills sound. On the twisting path, there is no light but that stolen from the far, dead moon.

"Yes, *Genipperteinga*. An unusual name. Old German. You have not heard of him? No matter. I can outline his biography. The standard source—a sixteenth century pamphlet written by a certain Casper Herber—tells us that he was born near Cologne, around 1540, and remained in that region until his death in 1581. A short life, even by the standards of the time. But the nature of his trade was not conducive to longevity. You see, Genipperteinga was a robber and murderer; in fact, worse, for—according to Herber—he was a cannibal, a witch, a contractor with the Devil.

"Now, whether you believe every element of Herber's somewhat, ah, *embellished* account or not, it is certain that Genipperteinga was a prolific, brutal murderer. He was not, perhaps, responsible for the nearly one thousand murders that Herber claims, but he certainly had scores of victims. And he seemed to take particular delight in killing children. There are lurid accounts of him hanging their bodies in trees; taking unborn babies from mothers to make magic candles from their fat; and so on ..." Aebersold looked at his feet, shaking his head slowly, as if bemused by evil's quirks.

"Why do such people exist, Isobel? My own view is that their development requires very specific combinations of nature and nurture. Probably, Genipperteinga's background was similar to that typical of the terrorists and serial murderers of today: abused as children, as adults these unfortunates express their unhealed pain by repeating and amplifying what was once done to them. It is as if they need to say to the world: Look! Do you know what happened to me? *This* happened to me! And this! And this! They start, often, with low-level abuse of one form or another; but the relief it gives them is only temporary. Their pain is never fully healed, and so they escalate their violence, further and further, continually seeking a solace, a justice, an *accounting,* that can never come."

Christman speaks. "When I was a child, Papa played such music as made my little bones dance. Oh, how he beat the time."

Somewhere, an old wind blows. Somewhere, memories break and bleed.

"Dance on! Dance on! Such a pretty game ..."

"Had Genipperteinga never been caught, I have no doubt he would have continued torturing and murdering until his natural death. But he *was* caught, back in the Germany of 1581."

Aebersold paused. His brow worked as though to fold recollections in flesh.

"They took nine days over his execution. They began by tearing strips from his skin and pouring boiling oil into the wounds; next they basted his feet in pig-fat and roasted them over a fire; then they broke his bones on the wheel, over several days; then ripped away his genitals with blacksmith's tools; and finally, they disembowelled him. Yet Genipperteinga's sense of injustice—his sense of his *own* victimhood—was such that, with his last breath, he screamed 'Murderers! Murderers!' at his tormentors. He sought not justice for his victims, Isobel, but justice for *himself.*

"For him, you see, those who administered his punishment were no different to those who had brutalised him as a child—those who had, in effect, killed the child and let something else grow in its place. They *still* had not understood his pain, that searing, unforgiveable, unhealable suffering that he had felt compelled to express through the pain of others."

Aebersold stopped speaking. His characteristic grin had disappeared; he looked at his own hands, with a small frown. Abruptly, he balled them into fists and raised them up; Isobel flinched and half-raised her own hand. But Aebersold did not notice.

"This is the problem when you mistreat children. They grow up, and *yes* their wounds have grown scars, and *yes* their broken bones have grown together, but inside each child there has grown a monster that must be fed. It *must* be fed."

Silence grew; Isobel felt increasingly uncomfortable. Eventually, she asked: "Monsieur Aebersold? Is there anything else?"

"Just one thing. As I said, Herber's account is quite well-known. Far less well-known is that Herber made a cast of Genipperteinga's face soon after his death. This I acquired some months ago; there is a market for such things, for those who know. And what you wear at this moment, is, of course, an exact replica of that death-mask."

Aebersold paused, head up, and smiled at Isobel, or rather, at the mask she wore. She raised her hands and felt the mask's features, but her fingers could not read her new face.

"And that, Isobel, is all I need to say, at this point. So, unless you have any questions, you are free to join the Masquerade. I repeat: as my guest, you may do as you please. Walk the maze. Sit beneath the trees. Find an anonymous lover, if that is what excites you. Or, if you are cold or tired, there is a fire and seating in the folly. Only do not remove the mask. That's all—*do not touch the mask*." As Aebersold looked at her, his smile faded; without it, his face seemed false and lifeless. "Remember, I shall be at the Masquerade too. In one guise or another."

∽ℚℚ ℚ∾

"They broke me," says Christman. "In so many ways."

They are at the maze's centre. All their world is still.

"Such pain," says Christman.

The child is silent.

∽ℚℚ ℚ∾

The drawing room also had French windows; Isobel walked through these and into the garden. It was dark enough now for torches to have been lit; they delineated a long, broad path, like a gallop, from Aebersold's mansion to the lake. Their smoke had an oily, chemical tang that penetrated Isobel's mask. People were gathering at the lake's shore; she could see stalls, bright lights and music. Perhaps she should just go to the folly. Two magnificently dressed women were heading in that direction, their gowns reflecting the torchlight as if covered in glass beads. What had Aebersold said? *Find an anonymous lover, if that is what excites you*. Well, perhaps she would; yes, perhaps she would.

Lord Peacock sailed past her, smothering Isobel's quiet 'Bonsoir' with the iridescence of his feathered cloak. A gaudy Colombina's half-mask showed off a privileged sneer; a Gnaga, in a dog mask instead of a cat, growled and offered her the contents of his basket—twists of paper containing who knows what—before whisking it away with a flounce; and a white-cheeked, red-lipped Arlecchino, bright as a circus clown, placed a hand on her breast and bent down to murmur vulgarities into her ear before pushing her away with a laugh.

In the Masquerade, Isobel realised, just as in life, those with power—money, and what money

can buy—do as they wish to those without. *Buy us, break us, throw us away*. Behind her mask, in her Morlock robes, she was just as much an unmoneyed nobody as she was when sitting unmasked on a Geneva tram. Just as unvalued as she had always been; always. Her eyes felt hot. Her fingernails cut into her own palms.

∽ℚℚ ℚ∾

Christman leaves the maze. And now Christman's sleeve is bare of ribbons, bereft of blue.

At the lake-side entertainments, a man sitting at a table addresses the crowd through a PA system. Mostly he delivers ribald commentary on the entertainers; now, for example, he mocks Harlequin and scorns the contortionist.

Christman leans over the table. Christman speaks.

As Christman leaves, an amplified voice echoes from lake to house: *Message for Eloise's mother— Eloise was feeling tired and has gone home with Auntie Beatrice. All is well.*

∽ℚℚ ℚ∾

"Congratulations, ladies and gentlemen, on persisting with our experiment until the end!" They were in Aebersold's office again. "And now the debrief. I regret, I have not been *entirely* honest with you ... but it was necessary. First, however, let us remove the masks. If you will permit—" Aebersold went to each of the four in turn, broke the wax seals and untied the cords that fixed their masks in place. They pulled their hoods back and took off the masks. Isobel turned hers around immediately: what did he look like, this Genipperteinge?

Aebersold clapped with pleasure. "And here is the first surprise, my friends! You were all wearing the *same* mask—and it was the same mask as that worn by all the other 'grey-robes'!" He held them up; indeed, all four masks were the same cheap, standardised plastic Carnival face.

Suddenly, Isobel understood. *Nothing changes; nothing ever changes.* She watched Aebersold: his cruel smile, his hard eyes. *The bastards. It's always the same. We are only here for their amusement; not ours.*

"Why? It was all part of the experiment, ladies and gentlemen. You were expressly given *carte blanche* to do as you wished during the Masquerade. And if this permission were not enough, your masks and costumes both disguised your true identity and gave you another, very specific identity. The idea was to see if, once liberated in this way, your respective psyches would tend to different behavioural patterns according to the mask you *thought* you were wearing. And you all thought you were wearing the death-mask of Herr Genipperteinge. All of you."

"As you will by now have guessed, there were others participating in this experiment; other groups of four who were told that they were wearing the mask of, say, Mother Theresa, or of somebody neutral."

Isobel pushed her hands—still cold from the February night—deep into the pockets of her cassock. She watched Aebersold; she thought about the wealth he had always enjoyed, the power he had always assumed as his right. *People like that think they can do what they want—to anyone.* Something rose inside her, some fury of injustice.

"Very interesting, but it's late. Is there anything else you need us for?" This was from one of the men; his voice was sharp.

"Only this: in order to test our hypothesis that certain cues will release certain types of personality to reveal the true self that they may keep hidden from all, even from themselves, I need to know about how you *felt* and *behaved* this evening. Data from the micro-recording devices sewn into your hoods—yes, another little surprise, Isobel, but don't worry, if you found a lover, my dear, we shall be discreet!—those data will be analysed and compared with the results from the personality tests you took last week. But before that, I need to hear from each of you about your *subjective* experiences. Did you feel that you were *enabled* in any way? That any of your normal inhibitions had been lifted by the death-mask of Christman Genipperteinga? Isobel, let's start with you."

✄ᓂ ᓂ✄

In Isobel's pocket, her hand winds the blue ribbon around her fingers, over and over, round and round. She starts to laugh, but the laugh dies. And then she takes a deep breath, so deep it seems her lungs will burst, and screams back to the very depths of her tortured, broken childhood.

"Murderers!" she screams. "Murderers!"

FICTION

FERAL

by Catherine MacLeod

D addy used to say, "The land reclaims." You wouldn't think the plainest truth in the world would need repeating, but he said it so often I got sick of hearing it.

These days, though, Daddy's mantra earns me a living. My agent charges unthinkable sums for my pictures and sells them all.

I photograph feral houses: buildings being reclaimed. Ghosts of their former selves, clinging to the memory of life with everything they've got. Vines tearing down brick chimneys; moss rotting shingle roofs; trees growing up through floors, shattering them slowly. Abandoned homes trying to keep their dignity in the face of inevitability.

I'm sure Mama would approve, because she taught me to tell the truth. And I'm sure Daddy would disapprove just because he could.

Feral: something domesticated returning to a wild state. They both had a clear understanding of that.

Some of my buyers make maps, tracking down the houses in their photos by using other clues in the picture—a distant mountain, the shine of a far-off river, even the position of the moon. It's not the safest hobby, but I can't criticize—I've done my share of trespassing, too.

But I'm not trespassing today.

There used to be a road here. Probably the last person who drove on it was Sheriff Tyler, coming up to check on Daddy. Likely the last person to walk on it was me, coming down to this not-much-to-look-at town and seeing no reason to stop. Now the only way you'd ever know there was a road is if you remembered. The land reclaims, and you get no say in the matter.

"I knew you'd come crawling back," says a voice in my head.

Daddy, however, *always* has something to say. Haven't heard his voice for a while. Can't say I've missed it.

But I've missed morning on the mountain something fierce. The leaves open like cool fog, and the wind is sweet. I'm a city girl now, but I'm always aware of the earth under the asphalt. Of land and urbanites fighting for space, both knowing who's going to win.

I was so determined to get off this mountain, out into that world.

"How determined *are* you, girl?" Daddy asked the one time I mentioned it, and I knew I should've shut my fool mouth.

But there was nothing to do but fight back. "Pretty damned," I said. And then, because he'd hated it when Mama said it, I added, "Pretty damned damned."

He kept forgetting I remembered her. She died young, and she had to have been willful, because how else could she have lived with him? But even he had to admit that when it came to stubbornness, she couldn't outdo me.

"There's nothing for the like of you out there," he said.

"Nothing here, either."

"Well maybe I should explain a few things to you."

But he didn't. Saying that was just a habit by then. Too many of his explanations had left bruises, and once he'd hurt me bad. That time had scared even him, and after that he didn't try to explain anything else.

He couldn't stop being mean, though. He'd always maintained control any way he could. He used to say, "You best make your peace with what you can't fight." I still can't imagine why Mama loved him, but she must have. I never had to imagine her loving me, though. I always knew it was so. She fed me well and kept me warm. She taught me to read and do math from the hundreds of books stacked around the house. She taught me to tell the truth.

Daddy lied when he said I could never leave here.

"I did the best I could," says the voice.

"Shut up, Daddy."

I'm not sure how long I've been gone. I haven't counted the years. But I have a right to be here now.

I've come to get what Daddy should've given me.

⊹∘ℂ ℂ∘⊹

The land reclaims. The U.S. has 20 million feral houses and 3800 ghost towns to prove it.

And, of course, the man Daddy killed.

We were filling our buckets from the river when he stepped out of the woods. He looked stocky and strong, and Daddy was on him in a second. He knifed him deep and said, "Take his bags to the house, girl."

At the time I didn't know the word *epiphany*. Up here, being ready to strike out at a moment's notice isn't a bad thing, but the man hadn't done anything but look surprised, and Daddy had still offed him like a snake. I remembered once, Daddy asking Mama, "Why would you want to leave here? You know people are no damned good." And her saying, "Does that include me?"

As Daddy dragged the man away, I realized he just didn't know how to deal with anyone who wasn't him, and maybe in his heart he never had.

I hauled the man's bags to the house and looked through them quickly. He'd packed three good knives, a handgun, and some camping gear. There was food and bottled water, which Daddy dumped out later because he said bottled water was poison, and money, which I'd never seen before. There were six magazines, five of them survival guides. I doubted they'd tell me anything Daddy hadn't already.

But the sixth was different. I'd read about a penthouse in one of Mama's books, but apparently there'd been some information left out. Were there really places where those skills were necessary for survival? I was wondering where they might be when I heard a car coming.

Daddy walked back into the yard as Sheriff Tyler parked. I stayed out of sight, like Mama taught me when I was little. She'd said the sheriff might try to take me away if he ever saw me. I hid the man's packs in case he came inside, though he never had.

The sheriff said, "Hello, Travis." The use of his name was the most familiarity Daddy ever allowed him. He'd never walked him around the property or showed him Mama's grave. "You have any trouble here lately?"

"Got a few more bear than I'd like. Why?"

"Because the richest woman in the county got murdered yesterday, and her handyman took off with the money. Couple of kids said they saw him on the road up here."

"Somebody killed Adele?"

"No, she passed years ago. She was never the same after her oldest, Christine, ran off. The guy killed Adele's youngest daughter."

"Marcy?"

"Yeah."

"Huh."

Somehow it had never occurred to me that Daddy was *from* someplace, or that he'd actually known people before he rejected them all. I couldn't imagine him anywhere but here. He said, "Nobody's been here since your last visit, and it's a hell of a long walk. Not to mention the bear. I'm not expecting any company."

"Watch out anyway, okay? He's considered armed and dangerous."

Daddy gave him a look. The sheriff gave it back. Daddy watched him drive away.

"Did you bury the man?" I asked.

"I rolled him into the ravine. He had no business being on my land." He was probably talking about the man and the sheriff, too. I doubt Daddy ever really owned that land. I know he never paid taxes.

I looked around as Daddy went through the man's bags. The house was clean enough. Mama's books were piled neatly here and there. The shelves were lined with jellied something and pickled whatever. It was home, but still... Daddy had seen other places; he had a hell of a nerve telling me I couldn't.

I left that night, after he fell asleep. I didn't want to feel obliged to say goodbye to him. In my heart I'd been saying it for years.

༺ ⚙ ⚙ ༻

The land takes back what belongs to it, and everything does. Given enough time, nature will tear down your cities.

But I want to see them all before it happens.

It took a week to find my first, and I walked non-stop, marvelling at things I'd only ever read about. A week after that, when I finally sat still, I met Derek Harris, the man who literally gave my life focus. I was outside a coffee shop, sipping something called latte and not liking it much, when he walked over and said, "May I take your picture?"

"Yes." He motioned me to the end of the nearest bench, posing me beside a wooden tub full of blue flowers. He took the photo, then flipped out the little viewscreen to show me. "You're very beautiful. Are you a model?"

"No." The picture was startling: I'd never actually *looked* at myself before. Daddy had taken down all the mirrors after Mama died. Maybe he didn't want me to be vain. Or maybe he couldn't stand to look himself in the eye. My hair was long and silvery blonde, my skin fair, my eyes so blue.

"You could be stunning if you wanted to be," Derek said.

I asked, "Are there any more pictures in there?"

There were. He said he hadn't shown them to anyone yet, but he was working on a series of photos of feral houses. I'd never heard that expression before, but when he showed me, I understood. "The land reclaims," I said, and he nodded.

"When you say it like that, it sounds like the plainest truth in the world." He offered to show me how to use the camera. Maybe he was trying to win my trust to make me biddable, or maybe he was just lonely enough to enjoy the attention. I took it from him and snapped a picture of the tub. He looked at the viewscreen for a moment, then huffed a laugh as my subject became clear.

"This is excellent," he said. "But I'm not happy there are rattlesnakes this close to my favourite coffee shop."

"I only saw the one." It blended into the shadows almost perfectly. You could only see it if you knew what to look for.

After a while he took me to his apartment. He asked if I was homeless, a word I didn't understand then. I said no because I had a home, I just didn't want to go there. His place was nice but not fancy.

He was a professional photographer, he said. He told me a photograph is a picture of your soul, which I know now is what people call a line. But that doesn't mean it's not true, even if some souls don't photograph well. He showed me hundreds of his pictures. Then he took me to bed and taught me the skills used by people in penthouses. I was awkward, he was gentle. I think I loved him a little bit by the time he was done.

When he fell asleep, I went to look at his shelves. He had coffee table books with photos of ghost towns and abandoned buildings, pictures that felt like pieces of my soul even though I hadn't taken them. I read all night. He died before sunrise. Even now I don't know what happened. He never said anything about being sick, and if he felt pain when we were joined, I couldn't tell. I've always wondered if it was something about the way I am. I haven't bedded anyone since, just in case.

I didn't call for help. Maybe Daddy's paranoia about law enforcement was more ingrained than I knew, or maybe at the time I just didn't realize I should—on the mountain when something was dead you just stepped over it.

I took his camera and a few of his books, and when someone tried to grab me in the parking lot, I broke his arm and watched him run. Not too different from life on the mountain, I thought—when you're attacked, you either kill the animal or make sure it's too scared to come back. Cities were just a different kind of wild.

But living in them would still require adaptation. Everyone I'd met had a job of some kind; it took me no time to choose mine. I had a good eye; I knew how to see what I was looking at. I'd use what I'd learned from Derek and my parents to tell the plainest truth in the world.

Which is what I do now. It wasn't easy at first, but I learned that kind words can open doors for you, and please and thank-you go a long way. I still heard Daddy in my head, saying I was foolish to think I might ever be somebody, but soon enough his voice faded and mine took over.

I learned that sometimes the truth needs to be flexible, and people are fascinated by beautiful destruction—which is how I met the editor who published my first book. His secretary had endless questions about my photos and why people would abandon their houses. I talked about the expense of repairs and upkeep, and access problems such as road closures, land disputes, and trouble with the bank. About places where jobs were vanishing so quickly the residents couldn't sell or rent, so they just walked away. I thought I was doing okay, until she asked, "What's your name?"

And I didn't know. Daddy only ever called me *girl*. But she was waiting. I glanced at the flower arrangement on her desk and said, "Rose Travis."

She wrote it in her appointment book, and I stewed about it until the interview. Daddy had never told me my own damned name, and I'd never thought to ask.

My made-up name suited the editor fine, though, and when I told him I had no ID, he was understanding and helpful. Apparently, the word *homeless* makes some people feel protective.

I never used Derek's photos. That would be stealing. But I still have them, and I think about him every day. I like the city, though I spend a lot of time out of it. Sometimes I get far off the beaten path, but I don't get lost.

I live almost like normal people, and that's fine.

But it's nice being back here, where I can stop pretending for a while.

ॐ ॐ

Daddy's house has gone feral and taken him with it. He's in what used to be his bedroom, his bones clean and his clothes shredded. Alders have grown through the walls, winding branches through his ribs. There's no point in burying him, he's halfway in the ground already.

The headstones out back are still intact, Mama's right beside mine. She was Christine Rachel Travis. Huh. I didn't know Travis really was Daddy's last name.

And mine. I am Elizabeth Adele. I never thought to look at my own stone. Though it's not as if I ever used it for anything.

Daddy taught me to survive. To live no matter what. He was a good teacher, but I know he didn't appreciate how well I learned. I take one more look around. This place is the one piece of my soul I won't photograph. This house, clinging to the memory of life with everything it's got. I won't forget what it looks like, and I don't want anyone else looking for it.

I don't know if I'll end up back here when I'm through living. When I finally face the inevitable. I'll make peace with that when I have to.

But I'm pretty damned determined it won't be today. I'm pretty damned damned.

It's the plainest truth in the world: the land reclaims.

But not yet.

FICTION

ADVENTUROUS

by Stephen Volk

Carole had wanted a nice house, big enough to grow a family in, nothing luxurious, not five bathrooms or anything ridiculous, just somewhere that looked nice, semi-detached, smart, not too old, not too modern, not needing a lot of maintenance, just somewhere 'comfy' as her mum would say, with a driveway to park in, one car, two at the most if she had a job as well, and a garage with one of those swing-up doors, though that could be used for storage, or an extra room, a games room for instance, with a billiard or ping-pong table for the kids, two of those, ideally, one of each, though she didn't really care either way, two daughters or two sons was acceptable, and a couple of wheelie bins with individualised numbers so that the neighbours didn't nick them, and a cat, or dog, depending what her husband felt about the subject. But, as it turned out, she didn't want any of it, not really.

As for husband ... well.

She never expected to get one with *Isambard* for a middle name. That should have got the old alarm bells ringing for a start. That, and his penchant for watching films about steam trains. Not any old films about steam trains, mind. They had to be certain journeys to certain destinations, and the length of the film had to be the *exact* length of the train journey, and it had to be shot from the point of view of the driver, without any cutaways, or there was no point.

She didn't think any of this as she gyrated on the dance floor at the Christmas party. She didn't think anything, much, or tried not to, as she flung herself at Roxy Music with abandon, not caring too much what Bryan Ferry thought, or Fergal "I-couldn't-possibly-be-homophobic" Daxter in his pink shirt, or that snooty cow *Deb-o-RAH* from the top floor, with her athletic knees and Comic Relief collecting box, face on her like she'd rescued the starving in Africa personally, one by one.

Carole's perspiration glued her dress to her body but she didn't care much about that, either, taking the opportunity to partake of the free booze, intending with no little gusto to get slaughtered under the multicoloured heat of the disco lights, which was when, propping herself for a much-earned breather at the buffet table, she noticed someone watching her. *Watching?* Was that too strong a word? Eyes in her direction, anyway. Eyes behind slightly askew glasses, too Specsavers to be stylish, pint held against his sternum, resting on the shelf of an incipient pot belly, the way men hugged their libations, more protectively than they ever did their wives. Top three buttons of his shirt undone, a sign of availability that was achingly desperate in a chap so young. Anyway, she went for it. Went for him. Heat-seeking. Mince pie in each hand, the two objects floating as if she was a child using them to mime a pair of flying saucers, till she stopped, swaying, trying not to look as pissed as she evidently was.

"Hello, you. I'm Carole. Have a mince pie," was her opening gambit, more an order than a request. Not surprisingly, the suit trembled.

"You're all right. Not keen on them, to be honest. Sorry."

She thrust one at his lips. "Go on, they're gorgeous!"

"No, no, really."

"Go *on!*"

The tin foil almost hit Colin Tweedie's front teeth and he recoiled into a green, unforgiving spotlight. Colin from Finance, originally from Potter's Bar. All the girls said he was a virgin, or gay, didn't have a girlfriend, lived with his mum, supported Arsenal, but Carole thought he was just shy, and she liked that. Better than a blabbermouth who thought corned beef of himself. He wasn't bad looking, she thought, if a bit spotty, and with a terrible Lego man haircut. And skinny. You could be skinny and a nice person, though, couldn't you? Sexy, even, at a push. It wasn't all about physical attributes anyhow, she told herself. She didn't want a stud. Some gym-addicted Adonis who'd ultimately have her crying into her pillow. What *did* she want? She wasn't sure. But she was still talking, and Colin, taller than her by about a foot, and younger than her by about ten years, wasn't listening, and neither was she anymore, the music being too deafening, as he squinted down at his watch and, bending over, lips close to her ear, had to shout he'd better be going home, like, and was sorry again, like, and she shrugged, mince pie filling her cheeks by now, flecking the crumbs from her breasts, turning away and returning to the dance floor, arms in the air.

Come the morning and Paracetamol, Carole saw him through the glass doors, gawky as a schoolboy. Straightened her back as he approached her desk past the other females, looking like a newly-conferred eunuch entering a harem. Carole wondered if he'd lain awake all night in his Arsenal pyjamas, surrounded by Arsenal posters and memorabilia, thinking about her, maybe even having exotic dreams of her nakedness, imagining her bare thighs, which in his dream would be smooth, muscled and tan, the stuff of an instant coffee commercial. Then the thought of masturbation on his part surfaced and she told herself to shut up. Even that inner reprimand, though imaginary, hurt her synapses and she cringed and hid her face. Rising from her desk, she walked to the stationery room, past her bitchy, small-minded colleagues who were probably thinking *virgin,* thinking *gay,* thinking *Arsenal supporter.* Colin followed restlessly, bending over to pick up a paperclip from the floor, examining it minutely as he said he wanted to email her but didn't know her surname, there were lots of Carols in the organization, and ...

"Car*ole*," she corrected, emphasising the *hole* part, realising as she heard it out loud that, with her dry throat from the night before, it sounded husky and seductive. "Spinks," she added, somewhat killing the illusion. She took a blue ballpoint from a fresh box and wrote down carole dot spinks at the name of the company dot com on a scrap of paper.

Colin, top row of teeth digging into his lower lip, stared at it in his hands as if it was a winning lottery number, or at least a scratch card, at least a possibility, at the very least that, as he backed away gratefully without another word.

Ten minutes later, an email. Subject line blank: *Hello! Would you like to go for a drink some time?—Colin.*

She typed *Yes,* but quickly deleted it. Didn't want to be too eager. Paused. Then wondered why. Why couldn't she be forthright? *Forthright.* She thought about the word. *Fourth.* What did the *fourth* part of it mean? And *right.* Was that *right* or *write?* She always got mixed up: was it *playwright* or *playwrite?*

She'd be it anyway, for once in her life, and wrote, impulsively: *Tony is up in Stoke tomorrow. All day. Not back till late. Come around at 2pm. This is the address.* She typed it, three lines, complete with the post code. Clicked SEND before she could change her mind, then waited nervously for a reply. To distract herself, she unwrapped the ream of paper she'd fetched from the stationery room and was bent over, replenishing the printer, thinking you could say he was *lean* rather than *skinny*—yes *lean,* she preferred that—when she heard a ping.

Got a meeting over lunch. Can we make it 3?

Her heart beating fast, she typed: *Great,* then deleted it with the backspace key and typed: *Fine.* Smiling as she typed excitedly: *I'll put the kettle on, and not much else.* Then deleted that with the backspace key and typed nothing.

⁓oᘏ ᘏoᘏ⁓

"I've, er, parked up the, er, road, just in case ..."

Colin wiped his feet on the welcome mat, his thought running out of steam. *Steam.* She wished she hadn't thought of steam. The big framed poster of the Forest of Dean Railway on the wall was more than enough. He stepped in front of it, over her son's muddy trainers and held up a bottle. She'd have sworn the lenses of his glasses were clouding; probably just him coming in from the cold air outside. Not his passionate ardour exud-ing from his biological interior.

"I didn't know if you like white or red."

It was white.

"That'll do," Carole said, tightening the belt of her dressing gown and fetching a corkscrew from the kitchen drawer, then dangling it from a hooked finger. "Bring it upstairs. Follow me. Sam's got football practice and Donna's got ballet lessons. We've got till about six. Is that all right?" Colin nodded. She looked for two glasses. "Good."

Twenty-seven, she thought, or twenty-eight, max. Living with his mum in Potter's Bar. In his room watching porn while his mum watches *Newsnight.* Was this his first time? Could be his bloody last.

She saw him looking around the room and wondered what he saw, what he really saw, what he made of it, what he made of her. The thirty-thousand-pound kitchen with marble work tops. The fridge magnets holding the kids' latest school reports in place. The old ginger cat that passed them as they climbed the stairs.

When the two glasses were empty, she closed the curtains, slipped off her dressing gown and got into the double bed. He turned away, not with any great meaning but to unzip and drop his trousers, making a mess of pulling them off over his shoes and socks. A six-year-old would have removed the shoes and socks first, which Carole told herself was an endearing lack of forethought rather than the sordid portent of disaster.

She watched him remove his shirt and put it on the back of a chair, over his jacket. She noted a bulge in his Marks & Spencer underpants. Eagerness to get on with it, she deduced. Her bare shoulders felt chilly. She wished she'd advanced the heating, which was set to come on at 3.30, but she hadn't. He had no chubbiness at all, other than two pouches above the elastic on his lower back, his pale Potter's Bar skin neither hairy nor hairless but sort of nondescript in the hair department.

He jumped into bed, and he was freezing too, making comic mileage out of his teeth chattering, which made her chuckle.

"This is nice," he said, and she said it was too.

"You're not intending to keep them on, are you?"

He peeled off said underpants and tossed them onto the carpet, lying next to her until she hooked her arm around his neck which he must have taken as a come-on, because shortly afterwards his body was on top of hers and his lips were on hers and dry. She took off his glasses and placed them on the bedside table.

"Now I can't see you. Now you're all blurry."

"My best feature," she said.

He kissed her again, wetter and with more suction this time. They were warming each other, gradually, but there was no hurry. She felt activity down between her legs. Saw him gazing deeply into her eyes as if expecting a verbal caution which didn't come. Instead, Carole, more from impatience than lust, guided his mouth to her right nipple, a movement which was accompanied, unexpectedly, by a piping voice from downstairs.

"Mr Macrae is off sick so we got sent home! Result!"

The slam of the front door juddered through her entire body and stiffened Colin—though not in the way Colin wanted to stiffen. He jerked up on straightened arms with a gasp. Quick as a flash upon hearing the thunderous footsteps on the stairs and the swiftly approaching "Mum? Mum?" he darted into the only place he could see, given he saw no lock on the bedroom door—no lock, no key. *Crap!*

"Mum?"

Colin stepped in and pulled the wardrobe door shut after him—

… Exactly as the bedroom door swung wide to reveal freckles, curls and the premature insouciance of an eleven-year-old.

"*Mum* … can I go round to Finlay's? We're going to do our homework together."

"Yes, that seems highly likely," Carole mumbled, elbows propping her up from the pillow, feigning being woken from sleep rather than *coitus interruptus*. "D'you … d'you want something to eat before you go?"

"No, his dad's outside in the car, waiting."

"Fine. Have a nice time." The door closed. "Text me when you want picking up."

"Okay!" The door opened again, half way. "Mum? Er … What are you doing in bed?"

Carole's eyes still hadn't opened. "I had a headache, and I didn't sleep well last night. I was up at four."

Shrug. "Okay."

The bedroom door closed again—with a finality this time.

Soon after, the front door followed suit, just as Carole's eyes fell on the clothes on the chair by the window—the suit jacket, trousers, shirt, tie. *Shit!* Her son hadn't seen them. The sudden, gut-hollowing sense of relief made her want a wee.

"Colin?"

No answer.

"It's all right, you can come out now."

Carole sat up on the side of the bed, bare feet with freshly painted toenails sinking into the beige carpet.

"Very funny. Don't play silly buggers."

Was he deaf or something, as well as being a virgin and/or gay?

"Colin?"

Annoyed now, she stood up, pulled on her dressing gown, and rapped the wardrobe door with a crooked finger.

Nothing.

The bottle of white sat on her vanity table. She uncorked it and refilled one glass. Good job her son hadn't notice *that* either.

"Two can play at that game. Cheers."

After a second mouthful, she shook a cigarette from her packet, lit it, but crushed it out in the ash tray without taking a second drag.

"Right. I don't know how you get your kicks, but this is not exactly a turn on. Not for me, anyway."

She turned the handle of the wardrobe and pulled it open.

As if he was leaning against it on the other side, Colin fell out, shoulder first—or, more like, was thrown out. Or, even more like—was running at full pelt for two hundred breathless yards and barrelled through the door with someone or something at his heels, to tumble, almost knocking her off her feet, then sprawled, panting, onto his knees, scrambling up onto her bed, gibbering.

"Bloody hell. Fucking *bloody* hell on a bike!"

"What?"

"*Shut it!*" Colin yelped, and she thought he was telling her to be quiet, till he added, pointing madly, jabbing his finger in the direction he'd come: "Shut the door!" So she did, as he wrapped himself in her duvet, backing as far as he humanly could into the corner. Away from it.

"Are you feeling all right?"

"No! Do I look all right? Fucking hell!"

His eyelids were pulled back, his face a polished surface of sweat, his hair lank and oily as if from a ten-mile run, his voice no more than a whimper, his vision fixed unblinkingly. Fixed on the wardrobe door.

"What's the matter?"

Colin didn't answer—huddled, shuddering like a man plucked out of an icy pond, but was laughing, as if the laughter was being hooked out of him with a spoon, or a pitchfork. It frightened her to death. Not least because he was turning aubergine. Her prospective toy boy was going puce.

"Are you having a heart attack?"

"I hope not."

"I'll call an ambulance."

"No! Don't you dare!" He swung his legs off the bed and shot to his feet. Pulled on his underpants with alarming speed and determination. (No bulge anymore, she noticed. Far from it.) "I need to go, I need to get out of here." He had his back to the wardrobe and shot a wary glance over his shoulder at it. "That place. They, they, they … What time is it? What *day* is it?"

"Wednesday."

"Oh, for fuck's sake."

"Have a drink." Carole filled the other glass with wine. "Calm yourself down."

"Calm down? You must be joking."

Nevertheless, Colin took it from her and sank it in one. And once he was dressed, he was gone. Carole didn't even get a chance to ask him to stay, if she'd wanted to. And she wasn't sure she did, she thought, as she rinsed the glasses and placed them back on the shelf where they'd come from. If he wasn't having a heart attack, what *was* he having? *Qualms?* A surge of disgust at what he was doing? At *her?* Was *that* it? Some elaborate way her frightened virgin, her Arsenal fan, who lives with his mum, to head for the hills, and not see her again?

Bloody funny way to do it, she thought, once she was alone with her puzzlement, but, then again, she never understood men at the best of times. Or was it some—what did they call it—psychotic episode? Maybe that. Or a stroke. Or brain embolism. In some ways, she wished it was.

In some ways, that would be a hell of a lot easier to understand.

⚘

Anyway, she didn't expect to hear from him again, but she did.

"Look," he said on the phone, with the surprising authority of a courage plucked up.

"What?" she snapped, curtly.

"Can I come round tomorrow?" More meekly, now.

She sighed, thinking she was an idiot for agreeing, but he sounded at a loss. He sounded desperate. And her husband was off again on one of his away days. And she could ring in sick again. So she did.

⚘

He cleaned his feet on the welcome mat even more vigorously the second time. She went on tiptoes to kiss him on the cheek. His eyes were fixed on the stairs.

"Can we …?"

Carole accompanied him to the bedroom. He gazed around it furtively, treating the wardrobe like an unexploded bomb.

After clearing her throat, she said: "Second time lucky."

Colin looked like he didn't understand the inference. She kissed him again, this time on the lips. His face showed total disinterest. He pretended otherwise but his eyes were continually drawn to the wardrobe.

She took off her top. He stripped to his underpants and socks, which were chocolate brown with lime green stripes. Daring for a man, she thought. Or perhaps she was out of touch with what constituted men's tastes, of late. She took off her skirt and hung it up on a hanger.

"I'm sorry," he breathed.

"Doesn't a man usually say that after sex, not before? This is a first."

His shoulders sagged, making his concave chest even more so. "It's no good. I don't expect you to understand. Nobody can. It's not possible."

"Try me, Colin."

"It's a duty now, okay?"

"What the hell are you talking about?"

"A solemn pledge. A mark of honour. Of, of chivalry, of … There's a girl, a woman, who—"

"And what am I, Colin? A lump of meat?" Carole sat on the bed in her not inexpensive, specially purchased underwear.

"It's not that." His face contorted with genuine conflict. "There's just something I've got to do. Can't you just accept that?"

It was pointless arguing. "Bloody do it then."

He'd looked troubled, and she couldn't bear that. The pity he wanted to extract from her that she didn't want to provide. She wanted to explain that to him, if she could, but it was already too late. He'd stepped into the wardrobe and closed the door after him.

Alone in the room, Carole put her ear to its door, her cheek to the mirror, but could hear nothing, not even the gentle rattling of wire coat hangers you might expect, if you expected a person to be in your wardrobe.

She sighed, remembering how Tony would tell her not to sigh like that, and ran a bath, which she thought might relax her, but it didn't, not really, though she became drowsy and her eyelids grew monumentally heavy, and she was starting to think of somewhere far away that was safe and nice and sandy and warm, somewhere they'd gone on holiday once, Sorrento or something, and she could almost smell the sun tan lotion when she heard a THUD from the bedroom and, eyes flashing open, wrapped in a bath towel, leaving wet footprints, she found Colin in a heap, the door of the wardrobe swung wide, and he was lying there in his socks and underpants, gasping like a big fish on dry land.

She saw cuts. Blood. She bent over him. Not cuts. *Claw marks.* Parallel. Four of them. Deep. Raked across his shoulder blade. *Gouges.*

"Heck! We need to get you to A&E!"

"No way. Get me some antiseptic and Elastoplasts, I'll be fine."

"What if you need a Tetanus jab?"

"It's not some rusty fucking *wire*, Carole. Jesus!"

"Pardon me for breathing."

"Well, don't. You have no idea." Touching his shoulder was a bad idea because it caused a jolt that ran though him like an electric current. His jaws locked. He hissed his words through a clamped wall of teeth. "That ... *fucking* thing! It won't die. No wonder they ... Jesus! It's incredible."

"What's incredible? Colin?"

"Everything!"

⚬ℚ ℚ⚬

Carole thought that would be the last of it and, to be truthful, part of her wanted it to be. Colin had been terse and rude and she didn't know where she was, in any shape or form, really, and didn't think it was fair. She hadn't asked for this, whatever it was, she really hadn't, and thinking about it was doing her head in. But two days later, just after lunch, an email pinged up, from you-know-who.

I'm sorry.

Carole stared at it for a minute and ignored it for a few more minutes, and even went for a cup of tea from the vending machine, and came back to her desk, before replying:

When?

⚬ℚ ℚ⚬

This time he wore walking boots rather than black business shoes, and a green anorak over his suit, the tail of the jacket extending two inches below its rim. His spine was straight and he didn't seem skinny anymore. The glasses weren't steamed up and his eyes were clear with resolve behind them. No, not resolve—*purposefulness,* if that was a word.

As Carole stepped aside, he carried in something long and wrapped in a blanket which she took to be either a fishing rod or golf clubs, being the only things she could remotely think of that would fit the bill. So when Colin unveiled a medieval broadsword on the living room carpet, it came as a bit of a shock.

"You're not bringing that in here. I have children in this house."

"Where?"

"Not now. Obviously not *now*. But generally."

"*Generally* doesn't matter. Not to me. Not with what I've got at stake, I promise you," Colin lifted the weapon in both hands, rehearsing a swipe or two in the air above a bowl of artificial fruit. "There's no alternative, see? Its scales are thick. Its claws are deadly. And if I don't get in there, well ... To be honest, I don't like to think *what* might happen."

"What are you talking about, Colin?"

He pressed the blade's tip into the floor and leaned on it like an umbrella. "The virgin! The Princess!"

"The who?"

He winced visibly at her inability to grasp the details. "Look, it *has* to be me. Don't ask me why, but that's what they all tell me. The prophecy says. The witches say."

"The what?"

"The wise women, priestesses, the oracle, the king, the chamberlain—everybody! The crowds in the street, thousands of them, the townsfolk, the peasants cheering."

"Cheering who? You?"

"Well, don't look completely astonished."

"Sorry. But, well."

He shrugged off her scepticism. "Look, they're all trapped in a state of fear. Terror. Frozen. Bewitched. No, not bewitched. Enchanted. Can I have one? I'm gasping."

She tossed her packet of cigarettes to him. Didn't know he smoked. Didn't know anything about him, actually. Apart from the *virgin/gay* business, and Potter's Bar, and his ambivalence on the hirsuteness front, and the Marks & Spencer underpants, which, now she added it up, was quite a lot to know about someone, actually.

He lit up, sucked in and breathed out, leaving little trails of smoke to come out of his nostrils. "It's lain waste the land. Devastated crops. Taken maidens every seven years. Ravished them. Eaten them. They thought they could satisfy its hunger, see. Do what it wanted. Ritual sacrifice, to save the city."

"Sounds positively medieval."

He gave her a long, hard, sour stare until the hurt of the remark abated. "It's got to stop. Don't you get it?"

"No. I don't. Why is this your business, all of a sudden? You're a young guy with a promising career in financial planning."

"Am I though? Am I *really,* Carole?" His eyes shone. Not his glasses. His eyes. "Thanks for the fag. I thought I'd given up. Spent a fortune on flaming NiQuitin patches." She took the ashtray with his dead cigarette stub and emptied the contents into the swing-topped bin. "Anyway, I'd better go. They'll be waiting." He looked over at the staircase.

"Do you need me to come—"

"No, you're all right."

He stood up, took his sword, which had been leaning against the washing machine, and went upstairs.

Carole settled on the sofa and leafed through a November 2018 copy of *World of Interiors* before switching on morning telly, which she didn't watch as a rule, as it tended to be wall-to-wall with middle aged Cockney men pretending to be chefs, or repeats of people going up the Amazon to find the world's biggest eel.

An hour later, when Colin arrived back, he didn't look well at all, and had a slight limp.

"It's worse than I thought," he said, wiping thick scarlet blood from his sword with some kitchen roll. "It has magical powers. And it's growing."

⁂

Carole felt bad that it wasn't convenient for Colin to come round to her house for some time afterwards. But not that bad. There was Christmas, after all, and, of course, New Year. Then, in January, her husband mentioned taking the kids to Disneyland Paris for the weekend. Going with his sister's kids in tow. Carole didn't get on with the sister, or the woman's obnoxious kids for that matter, spoilt brats who'd pulled her up on her lasagne at one point, so that was an easy thing to get out of, without too much obvious duplicity. Still, she was fairly ill-prepared for how Colin turned up on her doorstep that Friday evening.

She opened the front door to a vision.

Full suit of armour, white-plumed helmet with a visor, breastplate, the lot. Shield. Battle axe. Gauntlets. Chain mail. The full *Ivanhoe*.

Her first thought was to make a quip about fancy dress, but his expression very firmly told her—*don't*.

"I'm sorry, Carole," he said, eyes frozen with a conviction visibly tinged with abject terror. "There's no other way. I promise you there isn't."

⁂

Shortly afterwards he was sitting with her at the kitchen island, armour-plated feet long and pointed on the cross bar of his stool. Carole was a little worried his gauntlets might leave scratches on the black marble, which would make Tony hit the roof.

"Can I make you a coffee? I've just de-scaled the Nespresso machine."

"Go on then. Can't hurt."

Colin's plume bobbed slightly and his metal elbow joint creaked as he raised the tiny cup to his lips.

"Will you be careful?"

"As careful as you can be with a fire-breathing monster that weighs as much as fifteen double decker buses, Carole."

"No need to be sarcastic."

"Perhaps there is. Perhaps I need a little more support than someone undermining my confidence."

"I've never done that."

"Haven't you?"

Colin's mood shifted from tetchy to recalcitrant—again, with a degree of metallic creaking.

"I'm sorry. You're right. That was unfair." He shoved up his visor, which, irritatingly, tended to slip down over his forehead with a squeak. "I'm under a lot of stress at the minute."

She could see that. "Would you like a sandwich to keep you going?"

"No, ta. I think that's a bad idea. What do boxers have before a big fight? Raw steak. Bit of that might go down well. I'm kidding. I think if I had so much as a Twiglet I'd throw up." A little laugh salted the atmosphere.

"Colin, if I ask you something, will you answer honestly?"

He nodded. "If I can."

She wasn't sure if she should say it, but she did. "Are things going to go back to normal when all this is over?"

"I don't know. I really don't."

For all his faults, she did believe he was telling the truth when he said that, because he looked sad. Sorrowful. What's the difference between *sad* and *sorrowful*, she wondered? Except *sorrowful* sounded better. Almost like a good thing.

Halfway up the stairs, looking like a clanking astronaut ascending the ladder to his module, he paused and turned around.

"Goodbye, Carole."

"You haven't got a trusty steed outside, have you?" she joked.

"Don't be silly."

Carole smiled.

She couldn't help but follow him up to the bedroom, hesitating as she observed him in his contemplations before the wardrobe mirror. Sensing he was being watched, he looked back to find her standing on the landing.

"You know I have to, don't you?"

She nodded. "Wait a minute."

She knelt and looked for something in one of the drawers, wiped the dust off it, and hand it to him. It was a glove. A mitten she wore in winter. Something that kept her warm.

"Thank you," Colin said, tucking it behind the U of his breast plate. She could smell the metal tang of chain mail as he pressed his lips to hers and held her body to his.

Turning sideways to accommodate his battle axe and shield, he stepped, clinking like rattled saucepans, into the wardrobe, and she closed the door after him, carefully turning the latch to secure it, almost afraid to let go.

When she turned it back the other way and opened the door a second later, he was gone. She reached her hand inside, knowing what she would find.

Nothing.

Just her own clothes on hangers. No false panel. No door. No portal.

He was gone.

∾⊘⊙ ⊙⊘∾

Carole sat with her husband listening to tales of Disneyland. Of fairy tales. Of castles. Her children were excited, transported, and their happiness brushed off on her. How could it not? She wouldn't have been much of a mum if it hadn't. She enjoyed hearing their voices so much she held their soft hands as they talked, thought every syllable beautiful as a bird.

The weeks passed. Colin never reappeared.

The wardrobe became a wardrobe again.

In work, new rumours circulated. That he'd had a rich mistress. That he was married all along. That he was an international criminal. They asked Carole what had happened. She knew him, didn't she? "No," she said, "Not really. Not at all." But she thought of him every time she opened the wardrobe door. Thought of what he went to do, to save that land, that kingdom ... And over the next few weeks, and months, as the season changed colour and became renewed and supple again, the memory of him faded—but not completely ... *never* completely.

"Tony," she said to the man she'd married, as they lay in bed one night, reading separate books under separate reading lamps. "I want to move. Somewhere exciting. Not even exciting. Somewhere different. I want to *be* different. Both of us. We can, you know. We can, if we try, and we want to, if we want to enjoy life. Enjoy each other, like we used to. We can be ..."

She paused, just the way a television picture does when you press the PAUSE button.

"What?" asked her husband.

"... Adventurous," she said.

FICTION

A MOUTHFUL OF DIRT

by Maria Abrams

Interviewee: Clara Adler
Interviewer: [Name Redacted]
Location of interview: US Forest Service Rocky Mountain Regional Office / Drake, Colorado
List of acronyms: **CA**=Cara Adler / **IN**=Interviewer

[Begin Transcript 00:00:09]

IN: What's your relation to Jake Adler?

CA: Jake's my older brother.

IN: And it was Jake's idea to go camping?

CA: That's right. I fucking hate camping and those bags of rehydrated meats that are supposed to be dinner. You ever eat those? It's like eating a mouthful of hot dirt.

IN: Then why did you agree to the trip?

CA: I hadn't seen Jake in a long time. After our dad died, I moved out here. Jake stayed in Vermont. We both had a tough time with the death, but it hit Jake really hard. He didn't leave the house or return my calls. I can't tell you how many wellness checks I had to request to make sure he wasn't rotting away in that house.

A month ago, he calls me out of nowhere and asks if I want to go on a camping trip. When we were kids, he and I used to go each summer. Not far, only around the forest near our house. It was a way to escape.

Maybe he was feeling nostalgic or wanted an escape himself. Either way, I was just happy he was going to get out of that house for a while. So I agreed to go.

IN: Tell me about the first night.

CA: Uneventful. We drove to the campsite, set up, and went to sleep.

IN: You claim not knowing the campsite was on protected ground. Did Jake mention its location beforehand?

CA: No. He was in charge. He said that all I had to do was get into the SUV and relax.

IN: It didn't concern you? Not knowing where you were going, that is.

CA: Not at all. He was *so* excited, told me he had been planning it for weeks, and I trusted him. Like I said before, I hadn't seen him in ages, and he finally wanted to get out of that house.

IN: Tell me about the second night. The first time you heard the "strange noises," as you put it.

CA: It's true that Jake didn't tell me where we were going, but I knew we were in the backwoods and not a normal campsite; I'm not an idiot. So I also knew that we ran a greater risk of wildlife. I was ready to hear animals, but I wasn't ready for anything like this.

IN: Can you describe the sounds?

CA: Distant. At first. When you're camping, it's so quiet that you can practically hear the beetles chewing on the trees. It wasn't hard to hear the noises even from a distance.

It was like a whine, coming from something injured calling out for help. It started high-pitched, squeaky. A dog whine. Then it became deeper, more guttural. Coming from the stomach and not the throat ... moaning. That's what it sounded like, a moaning cry. After about ten minutes, it stopped.

IN: When you asked Jake about the sounds, what was his response?

CA: He said he didn't hear anything, but it was most likely a coyote and nothing to worry about.

IN: You didn't believe him?

CA: No. I know what coyotes sound like. This was no coyote. Coyotes don't sound like they have vocal cords.

IN: Vocal cords?

CA: Yeah. That was the thing with those sounds. You could almost make out words through the wails. Or at least something trying to form words.

IN: You said the noises continued the next night as well. Were they the same?

CA: Almost. The tone was, but they were closer.

IN: And then you found the prints?

CA: [Nods].

IN: Can you describe that morning when you found them?

CA: I barely slept after hearing the crying, so when I saw a sliver of sunlight, I stepped outside. That's when I saw the footprints leading into Jake's tent.

They looked human. Human, but barefoot. There were toes and a heel indent. But they were thin. Too long. I know some people have bigger feet, but I've never seen a person with feet this stretched.

Since they led into Jake's tent, I immediately panicked. I started calling his name and shaking the tent hoping it would wake him if he were inside. I was too scared to unzip it to see what was inside.

IN: But you eventually did open the tent?

CA: [Nods]. He wouldn't respond, so I had to.

IN: What did you find?

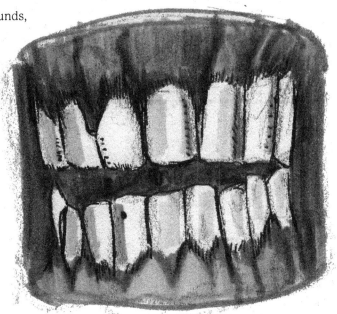

CA: A balled up pair of socks flying toward my face. And an angry brother wondering why I woke him up so early.

When I showed him the footprints, he wasn't bothered. He told me he must have gotten up to pee in the middle of night and left a track. I questioned him about walking around with no shoes on, which he wouldn't do. As you know, camping in late September means the ground is freezing. There's no way he could walk around barefoot without his feet stinging.

IN: Was Jake acting odd throughout the whole trip?

CA: [Pauses]. In retrospect, he was. I didn't think it at the time. In fact, I thought *I* was going crazy. Hearing noises, seeing footprints, none of which fazed Jake. No matter what I said or how freaked out I was, he had an excuse for why I was wrong. It was so...frustrating.

IN: Is that when you had the argument?

CA: It is. I was so tired and so cold, and all he did was sit there. Buried in his own thoughts that he refused to share. Not speaking to me at all, really. It was *his* idea to go on this stupid trip in the first place, and the least he could do was say something.

[CA inhales audibly]

That's when I brought up our father. I wanted to get a reaction, and I knew the topic would rattle him.

IN: What did you say?

CA: I reminded him that our father was a piece of shit who deserved to die. Those were my exact words. I know it sounds horrible, but you have to understand. Our father spent most of his life getting drunk on cheap vodka. And when he wasn't at the local dive bar, he was at home, beating the spit out of Jake. "Beat the ugly off him" he called it. He would say, "Jake, I'm doing this to make you a man. Beating the ugly off ya."

He was so angry, so full of hate. That man was the only true evil I have ever seen.

IN: Is that when Jake disappeared?

CA: [Nods and pauses]. He listened to my rant about our dad. Said nothing. And walked into the woods.

IN: Why did you wait until the next morning to leave the site and contact help?

CA: I...I don't know. I really thought he'd be back before sundown. When he wasn't, I didn't want to drive in the dark. The road we took in was rough and Jake's so much better at four wheeling than I am. I couldn't afford to get stuck or pop a tire.

At first light, I drove until I had a cell signal and called the police.

IN: Thank you, Ms. Adler. That's all we need—

CA: Wait. There's one more thing.

IN: Go on.

CA: The night before I left the site, the noises returned. This time they were closer. The other nights, it was definitely coming from only one... *thing*. But that night, there were two of them.

I couldn't move. I felt so trapped in that tent. The sleeping bag pinning me in place as I shook in a cold sweat. A rat in a trap waiting for the hungry cat.

The tent had a rain layer, so I couldn't see anything through the nylon. Not even a shadow. But I could hear one of them. Coming closer. Its guttural groan becoming louder, its feet slapping against the wet ground. Then it reached the side of my tent.

All I could see was its imprint against the fabric. It was breathing so close to me, that the material pushed in and out with each breath. Those, I could see. The condensation of its hot breath on the side of my tent.

The breathing was raspy, like it was struggling.

Before it tried to get in, the other one grunted, and they left. The next morning, the footprints were back. They led to the side of my tent.

I could see a ring about the size of a mouth. There was no saliva, just a circle of black. Mucky and thick.

[00:16 second pause]

IN: Is there...anything else you would like to add?

CA: [Shakes head].

IN: Thank you again. That will be all for now.

[End Transcript 00:12:41]

LOOKING BEYOND.

Nosetouch Press pushes genre boundaries
with dazzling design and stellar storytelling across
genres as diverse as fantasy and science fiction, folk horror
and supernatural, as well as weird fiction.

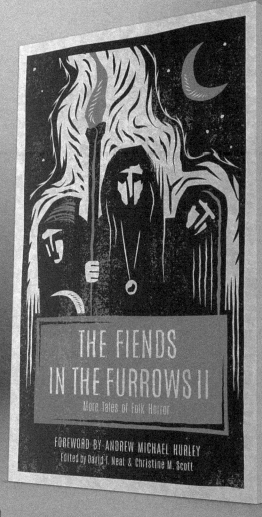

"*...All the stories are well written, with huge gobbets of terror and weirdness running through their veins.*"
—Alyson Rhodes, at Goodreads

"*I believe this is one of the best anthologies to come out in 2020.*"
—Christi Nogle, for *Pseudopod*

FICTION

THINGS FOUND IN RICHARD PICKMAN'S BASEMENT, AND THINGS LEFT THERE

by Mary Berman

Don't be a fool, Thurber. Of course I killed my husband. I suppose you thought Richard Pickman killed him, just because he paints monsters and he's got a house in the North End. I don't suppose you know that I grew up in the North End? Ah, that shocks you, doesn't it. Just imagine: A pretty young woman rising from the tangled shadowed alleyways and subterranean nightmares of the North End, and then insinuating herself among the upper class! The horror!

You're such a bore, Thurber.

What? Yes, I know about Pickman. You may not recall this—I expect the death of your good friend Eliot is overwhelming you, as you don't seem to be a man who handles stress very well—but a few days ago you paid a call to my husband, and I happened upon you gossiping about Pickman and his predilections and his North End house. I realized the house you meant at once. It's up on Snow Hill, the big mansion on the corner nearest the graveyard, not very far from Old North Church. It changed hands three times when I was a child. Now that Pickman's disappeared, I expect it will do so again.

Anyway, Thurber, you haven't asked me the most interesting question. Go on. I know you're dying to.

No. Not "What did I find in Richard Pickman's basement?" You imbecile. The real question is: Who else did I kill?

◦◖◔ ◕◗◦

I killed Susan, my husband's sister, first. This was only about a week ago. Believe it or not, I had never killed anyone before, although of course the thought had occurred to me. Doesn't it occur to everyone at some point? No? That's rich, coming from you. I understand you committed a number of murders when you were in the war. What do you mean, that doesn't count?

Anyway, Susan was visiting us from Providence. Really she was not so much 'visiting' as 'moving in,' no matter what my husband said. She was fresh off a divorce that had left her, let us say, delicate, which is to say she was a fucking nightmare. And since my husband, your dear Eliot, was always off at your little club, I was left to bear the brunt of her. Listen. If you'd had to put up with a week of this hoity-toity harridan insisting that you were a simpleton, slum trash, uncouth, frigid, unkempt, filthy, that your husband should have left you in the gutter where he found you, never mind that I met him when I was on scholarship at Radcliffe, an achievement that Susan could never have even... I'm sorry. I got distracted. My point is, you would have had to kill her too. One day, I brought her a plate of bread and butter, trying to make nice, and I found her crying. I suppose she was embarrassed, because she started ranting about how civil women understood privacy and manners, but of course the sluts in the North End didn't know enough to teach their daughters such things, and I put the plate on the end table and I just walked over to her and snapped her neck. Necks are surprisingly fragile, you know. Snapping one is more about momentum than anything else.

Well, then I was in a bind. Thank God my husband was not home. I dragged Susan out of the drawing-room and down the stairs and left the corpse at the base of the steps, right in the foyer,

so my husband would trip over it when he came in. I ate the bread and butter, put the plate back in the cupboard, and retired to bed with a cold cloth on my forehead. A while later the front door opened with a loud bang, the way it always did when my husband had been at the club. Then another bang, as of something very heavy stumbling and thudding to its fleshy knees. Then a restless silence. And then, at last, a strangled sound, halfway between a gasp and a scream.

When he finally fetched me, I told him I'd been in bed with a headache. I feigned astonishment at his shock and his news. Together we concluded that Susan must have simply fallen down the stairs.

᭶᭜ ᭜᭶

It was with my next murder that I made the mistake. No, you ninny, not my husband. We're not there yet. No, this one was the undertaker, Fitzpatrick. I saw him whispering to my husband during Susan's funeral, and it made me itchy. After the funeral my husband drove home with his knuckles white on the wheel, two furious red blotches burning high on his cheeks, and he would not answer me when I asked about his conversation with Fitzpatrick. It was clear to me that Fitzpatrick had seen evidence of murder on Susan's body. And he must have told my husband that I was the culprit.

Needless to say, when Fitzpatrick visited my house the next day, I was already in a state. My husband was not home; he was paying you a call, I believe. I met Fitzpatrick in the drawing-room, my mind working furiously. Perhaps I could stab him with the fire poker. Too messy. I could strangle him and stuff food in his throat. Too shoddy. I could—

"I'm so sorry for your loss," Fitzpatrick said.

I wondered why he bothered.

"I apologize for neglecting to offer you my condolences yesterday. You see, I was speaking with your husband."

I couldn't stand it. I had to get out of there before I ran him through with the fire poker. I pretended to be overcome with emotion, swiped my hand over my eyes and said I was running to the kitchen to fetch him some refreshment. He didn't pursue me. Perhaps he didn't think I would try to escape.

And he was correct. For when I was in the kitchen I saw the cleaning closet. In the closet was the arsenic we used for killing rats.

I put together a tray of bourbon, coffee, and cheese, and I supplemented the beverages with a hefty dose of poison. I rubbed my eyes until they reddened, and I returned to the sitting room. Fitzpatrick looked relieved to see me. He seized the bourbon gratefully and drained quite a bit more of it than was decent. "Mrs. Eliot," he said. "I'm afraid I've got something very unpleasant to discuss with you."

"Please do go on," I said blandly. I expected the poison to make him ill almost immediately, but I did not think he would actually keel over until later in the evening. (I was correct about this.)

"It's about your sister-in-law," said Fitzpatrick. "Forgive me. I recognize this is a deeply disagreeable subject. But the neck did not appear to have been broken by a simple fall."

I gave him nothing. If the man was about to clap me in chains, the very least I could do was make him uncomfortable.

Fitzpatrick took a deep breath. He said, "I think your husband may have murdered Susan."

"I beg your pardon?"

"Let me explain," said Fitzpatrick, but then his body spasmed once. He clapped his hand to his mouth. All at once he looked quite green.

᭶᭜ ᭜᭶

Fitzpatrick fled home to be sick in peace. I was on tenterhooks for two days. I finally learned of his death from you. You were in my drawing-room; you'd visited to tell my husband that wild story about visiting Richard Pickman's house in the North End, and seeing that damned photograph of the ghoul gnawing on a man's head, and so forth. I passed by the drawing-room to fetch a cup of tea. At that precise moment, you were telling my husband that Fitzpatrick had been found dead in his home the previous morning. That the coroner had determined that he'd died the evening before.

I paused.

You and my husband, the dear departed Howard Eliot, were facing the fire. Your heads were tilted closely together, the steep curves of your twin armchairs silhouetted by the low flames. I was enshrouded in the shadows of the hallway. I could not be seen.

"Heavens," my husband said. "What was the cause?"

"Poison," you whispered.

Both of you were very quiet. I was even quieter.

"I expect Pickman did it."

"Oh, for Pete's sake, Thurber —"

"You haven't seen his house in the North End." And you spun your wild tale.

At the time, I didn't believe half of it. (Now I know better, of course.) As I've said, though, I knew the house you meant. And I have to admit that listening to your conversation enraged me. I scorned you, both of you, for being foolish and snobbish and full of fear, for your terror at the prospect of leaving your ritzy art clubs and your clean-lined Georgian houses. At least Pickman, I thought, was not afraid. But then I thought about it some more, and I decided that Pickman was no better than my husband, no better than you. Pickman treated my childhood neighborhood like an amusement park. He'd purchased a house there exclusively for the purpose of slumming it for the shock factor, so he could horrify his friends at the club. I could not contain myself. I sucked in my breath with anger, and both of you heard me. You looked up. The expression on both of your faces surprised me. It was something very like fear.

Then my husband's expression coalesced into anger. He stood. He said my name.

You said you ought to be going, and you fumbled for your coat.

Ah. You do remember this. So you see, Thurber, it's not only my fault your friend Eliot is dead. It's your fault, too. You should have stayed.

My husband saw you out and returned a minute later to the drawing-room. I was waiting for him. I knew how this scene, by necessity, would play out. Frankly I rather relished it.

He demanded of me, "What's gotten into you?"

"What's gotten into me? What's gotten into Mr. Thurber?"

"Never mind Mr. Thurber. You disrespected me by eavesdropping on my private conversation. You embarrassed me in front of my good friend and a member of the club."

"Oh, you and the club." I'm not ashamed to tell you I snapped at him. I was still angry from your breathless, half-titillated description of the North End, and angry too with my blind, useless, spineless husband, who always spent half his time at the club and the other half with you and a decanter. "Thurber's too busy having a nervous break-

down to worry about you. He shan't tell anyone."

"Mister Thurber," my husband corrected me.

I did not say anything.

My husband said my name, loud and insistent and brash. Still I said nothing. I would not even look him in the face. I was so angry.

He came over to me and sank his fingers into the flesh of my upper arm. It hurt. "Answer me. Why were you eavesdropping on us?"

"Mister Thurber was talking about the demons in Richard Pickman's basement," I said evenly. "It isn't the sort of thing you overhear every day. I was interested." Note that I did not apologize. It's important to me that people know that.

"How long were you standing there?"

I did not answer.

"Did you hear us talking of Fitzpatrick's death?"

I did not answer.

"He died two evenings ago. Of poisoning."

"How terrible," I said.

My husband's fingernails made half-moons in my body. "You heard us. And Thurber said that Fitzpatrick was here, at our house, the day he died. That means he must have visited with you. And— and Fitzpatrick told me, at the funeral, that Susan looked like she'd had her neck broken."

"Why," I asked, very quietly, "don't you say the thing you want to say?"

My husband shook me. "You'd better tell me what you know right now."

"You'd better not order me around ever again."

"How dare you, you little—"

He had not accused me of the murders. Was he really so stupid that he couldn't put two and two together? Or did he not want to believe it? Or was he simply incapable of understanding that his young, pretty, soft, small wife, whose upper arm fit entirely in his grasp, could be a killer?

I did not care. I was beyond caring. This man would never be able to lay his hands on me again. With my free hand, I removed my hairpin and stabbed him through the jugular.

❧ ❧

After I cleaned up the blood and changed my clothes, I thought about where to hide the body. And at once I thought of your story about Richard Pickman. His house by the graveyard. The well in his basement.

But Snow Hill was two miles north. How would I get the body there? I couldn't exactly summon a taxi.

In the attic I found a great, wheeled trunk. We'd only used it twice, once when traveling to Europe in 1922 and then again last summer, when we'd visited Susan in Providence. I dragged the trunk down to the drawing-room, folded my husband up—I had to break some of his joints to make him fit—and stuffed him inside. Then I took his revolver out of his study and put it in my pocket, and I set off. I was a woman walking alone at night, you know. It was safer to have a gun.

I didn't need it, though, not until later. It was past midnight by now and I encountered very few people. Navigation was easier once I reached the North End. Even after all these years, the alleys of that neighborhood are as familiar as my features in the mirror. And the house, Richard Pickman's house, its gabled roof as impenetrable as the face of a mountain, its cracked windows hollow like eyes: That was familiar, too. I breathed a sigh of relief when I saw it.

The front door was locked, but the wooden doorframe had rotted through. I broke in easily. In the pitch-dark foyer I dropped the trunk and rested for a moment. For one thing, I was exhausted and sore—it's no joke lugging a grown man around Boston!—but for another I was trying to get a sense of my surroundings. It would be awfully rich if I made it all the way to Pickman's house and then broke my neck going down the stairs.

Eventually, when my eyes failed to adjust, I began feeling my way around the walls, searching for a doorway or a light switch. The walls were not wood or brick but some thick, flexible stuff. And then, what luck!, I found an oil lamp and a pack of matches.

I lit the lamp. I stared around.

Frankly, Thurber, when I saw that room, I understood what you'd been so hot and bothered about.

The walls were plastered with canvases. Pickman had painted great, black-furred beasts slavering in the graveyard by the house, feeding on long-dead corpses beside exhumed and open coffins. He had painted them stealing infants from their cradles in the night. Lots of shadows and rotting flesh and teeth. There was a whole series of a person with his own face, mutating into a fanged and vicious animal. In the center of the room was a massive portrait, very fresh, of a ghoul with a humanoid face and shambling gait. Each hair on its body was picked out with the delicacy of an eye-lash, and it was eating a human body like a lollipop. Was that the painting that sent you running for cover, Thurber? It was very easy to look at that painting and think that the monster was real. I remember wondering if it would have any interest in my husband's corpse.

At last I found the basement stairs. I thunked down them with my trunk. At the bottom, Richard Pickman was waiting for me.

For Lord's sake, Thurber, don't scream like that. You have to remember, I'd never actually met him before. To me, he was just a hunched, hollow-eyed, middle-aged man. Though he was standing with his feet spread in a fighting stance, and he was pointing a revolver at me.

I dropped the trunk instantly and grabbed my own gun. But Pickman was already lowering his. He frowned hard for a second, and then he said, "Mrs. Eliot?"

"You must be Richard Pickman," I said.

"...You are Mrs. Eliot?"

I did not see the point in answering this. I was looking around the cellar. It was brighter down here, with a number of lanterns and candles. The room was papered with sketches and works-in-progress, which were more or less as revolting as the paintings upstairs. Hanging on the corner of an easel was Pickman's camera. And there, in the center of the room, was the great crumbling stone well with its wooden cover.

Pickman put his gun down on the rim of the well and came toward me. I stepped back. My mind was working furiously. Evidently I would have to kill Pickman, but I could see that he was made of stronger stuff than my husband and Fitzpatrick and Susan. He would put up a fight. I tightened my hold on the gun.

A thump sounded from the well.

I tensed. Pickman whirled. He fumbled for something in his clothes.

The wooden cover slid half off the well, and a set of claws hooked itself over the rim. I had never seen anything like those claws. They were two inches long, gunmetal grey, smooth and curved like a cat's.

Pickman was still searching for something. Then he stopped. "My revolver," he said anxiously. It rested on the rim of the well, ten feet away.

An oblong, furred, humanoid head poked out over the claws. I saw a flat puggish nose, a wide mouth, a pair of eyes the color of hot coals. Then a lanky, skeletal body with ribs and a collarbone that jutted forth like pens or blades. The creature placed a single foot, long and flat like a wolf's paw, on the rim of the well. It bared fangs—and Thurber, those fangs ought not to have fit in its mouth. And they were dripping, thick with saliva and maybe blood—

I screamed—it's embarrassing to admit now, but what can you do—and I shot it in the neck.

The animal—animal?—howled and careened backward into the well. My muscles were coiled like springs; I could hear nothing but the sound of my own blood. I strained for the sound of the creature's body colliding with the well bottom, but I never heard it.

Pickman exhaled shakily. Then he rounded on me and shouted, "What are you doing in my house?"

Well, I felt that the fact that he was hiding a monster in his basement changed the terms of the game somewhat. So I told him. "I'm disposing of a body."

"I beg your pardon?"

"I killed my husband. I killed his sister Susan and Fitzpatrick the undertaker as well, while we're on the subject. Pickman, what is in that well?"

"Mr. Pickman, if you please, Mrs. Eliot."

"Christ almighty," I said. I pocketed the revolver and, ignoring Pickman, dragged my trunk over to the well. But when I peered cautiously into it, I saw nothing but darkness. I dropped the oil lamp, hoping it would illuminate the bottom of the well when it broke. Instead, it vanished into the shadows.

Pickman came and stood next to me.

"Where does it go?" I asked, unable to help myself.

Pickman hesitated. Then he said, "It leads to Carter's Dreamlands."

Thurber, does that mean anything to you?

Me neither. Still, I imagined it was probably difficult to track a dead body there. I unbuckled the trunk and hoisted my husband out of it. His broken limbs dangled like cut strings.

Richard Pickman reared back from me in horror.

I heaved the body over the edge of the well and watched it fall. And that was that.

I turned and met Pickman's eyes. He was staring at me uneasily, having turned away from me slightly as from a hot fire. It's true, you know, that there's something queer about his features. And his shoulders are rather too hunched, and his gait too shambling, even for an aging man who spends half his time bent over a canvas.

In a rather wondering sort of tone, he said to me, "You look human."

"I should hope so," I said stiffly.

"So you aren't... You haven't been to..."

I waited.

Pickman rubbed a claw-like hand over his thinning hair. At last he said, "Mrs. Eliot, you cannot dispose of your corpses in my basement."

I looked at the canvases, the yawning well, Pickman's weird shifting face. I asked, "What are you going to do about it?"

Richard Pickman said nothing.

I left.

⁂

Well, I never made it home, of course. Someone had heard the gunshots and called the police, who were gathering outside. They saw me staggering out of the old house with filth and bloodstains on my dress. They brought me in for questioning, and someone realized my connection to Susan and Fitzpatrick. And here I am, in a cell.

But guess what, Thurber? They're going to let me go. I blamed everything on Pickman. I left the gun and the bloodstained trunk in his house, thank God, and Pickman disappeared after I left his basement, so he's not around to claim they aren't his. The police went inside to investigate and saw the paintings and the weapons and the well. Such horror. Such strangeness. Everyone believes he did it.

But here's the real reason they're going to let me go: I'm young and pretty and soft and small.

Yes, I know I've just confessed everything to you. But I'll ask you the question I asked Richard Pickman: What are you going to do about it?

Go on then, if you want to. Tell them everything. But I know you won't, because you want them to catch that twisted old man. You're more afraid of him than you are of me. Even with the story you've just heard, you think you've got more to fear from an artist and his ghouls than from a young woman with a hairpin and a trunk. You poor, dear, stupid man. You've got a lot to learn.

FICTION

BONEMILK

by Rob Francis

The old woman was mostly covered by a thin off-white bedsheet, so that only her head and feet protruded. Her grey hair fanned out across the dark farmhouse table she lay upon as if it had been carefully arranged. Her face, or what remained of it, was terribly withered and wrinkled, flattened as if the skull itself had crumpled to nothing. Two tiny, desiccated eyeballs stood out from the mess. Her feet appeared much the same, flopped over at the other end of the sheet like a pair of broken slippers.

Derek stood in the cabin doorway for a long time, mouth open, breathing in dust, his hand still resting on the door handle. The last time he'd seen a dead body had been that of his old man, over forty years ago. That hadn't affected him all that much—had, indeed, allowed him to inherit the family home and set him on his path as a property developer and landlord—but he'd always imagined stumbling across a corpse unexpectedly like this, and on his own land no less, would've provoked more of a reaction. On the other hand, it wasn't like he *knew* the woman. And above all, Derek Broome was *pragmatic*. A successful career demanded it.

He stepped back from the garden cabin and stared across the lawn at Glynwood in all its Victorian splendour. He'd been living in the renovated farmhouse for three months now, largely ignoring the garden and outbuildings until the Black Mountain winter had passed. Had *she* been on the property all that time?

It was the most likely explanation. Terry, the local contractor Derek had hired, had locked the cabin back in November and mailed Derek the only keys, at least as far as he knew. And this was the first time he'd opened it. Had Terry left the woman here, like this, knowing Derek would find her?

A cold breeze swept across the valley that lay beyond the edge of his property, icy fingers creeping under his coat and down his neck. The garden offered a superb view of the Welsh hillsides with their dark patchwork of scrubland and hedgerows. It was the kind of panorama he'd always wanted to feature in his retirement. He'd earned it.

Call the police, that was the thing to do. He'd done nothing wrong. Perhaps a stiff drink first, to warm himself. A glass or two. She'd clearly been there for some time, so another hour or so while he composed himself wasn't going to make much difference. He'd taken a step towards the house when a faint rattling came from inside the cabin.

He paused.

The cabin was big. As spacious, certainly, as some of the studio apartments he rented to young professionals in Islington and Camden at very reasonable rates. Small in comparison to the garden it stood in, and the farmhouse itself, but still. Big enough to hold more than a corpse on a table.

Derek swallowed. Carefully, so as not to pull a muscle or trip his back, he lowered himself to the ground to peer under the cabin, which stood on a flat expanse of soil, the wooden structure mounted on a short stand to elevate it above the wet earth. Nothing. Only dead grass and shadows.

He clambered to his feet and stepped back inside. Pale winter sunlight illuminated the cabin interior. The corpse drew his eye again, and he was struck by how the body didn't seem to be particularly *decomposed*. Just dry and empty.

The rest of the cabin was occupied by bits of furniture that Derek had shipped up from London—though not the farmhouse table, he realised—and which he intended to sort through with an eye for resale. He moved into the gloom of the cabin, pushing past chairs, chests and cupboards, moving from window to window to check if any were open. Was that where the rattling had come from?

He was carefully checking a window latch, his attention entirely focused on it, when the child stepped from behind a chest of drawers. Derek was so badly startled that he crashed over a stack of chairs and landed painfully on the wooden floor, jarring his elbow.

The child was small, no more than two feet tall and stick-thin. Its skin was the translucent white of apple-flesh, and it appeared entirely hairless, with a bare scalp and no eyebrows or even eyelashes. It wore only a long white t-shirt and faded green shorts. Derek couldn't tell if it was a boy or a girl.

"Jesus," he said, heart racing, the tickle of dust in his throat making him want to retch. "What the hell are you doing in here? This is *my* cabin."

The child frowned and licked its lips, the light pink tip of its tongue there and gone again.

"Waiting," it said, its voice high and piping. "I've been in here for a long time. It's good someone finally came."

Derek struggled to his feet, pointedly rubbing his elbow. The child offered no sympathy.

"Where are you from?" Derek asked. "Do you live somewhere nearby?"

The child frowned again. "I live out there. In the hills, with the others. Don't you know? You're *old*."

Derek ignored the question. He'd lived long enough to justify disregarding anything that didn't make sense to him. Sadly, it seemed to be an ever-growing list.

"Who's this?" He pointed to the old woman. "Your grandma? What's she doing here? This really isn't on, you know." He sighed. "I'll have to go phone someone. How far away is your house?"

"I'm glad you came, because I'm hungry."

Derek shook his head, dismissing both the child and the situation. "I'm going to make a call. Come with me, and I'll get you something from the kitchen. The police can take you home."

The child narrowed its eyes. "I need milk."

"Yes, I have milk in the house."

The child screwed up its face in distaste. "Not *cow's* milk. Bonemilk."

"Bonemilk?"

It motioned towards the old woman. "Bonemilk. Isn't that why you came? You're *old*. You've nursed those bones for a long time, made them rich with age. Time to pass them on. Make use of them while you can. Give something back." The tongue flashed again.

As the child stepped closer, Derek caught the sour scent of spoiled milk.

Derek had never had children, or much to do with them, but even he was sure this wasn't how a child was supposed to behave.

"What *do* you think you're doing?"

"I'm hungry. You're supposed to give freely. We can only live on what we're given, now the land isn't ours."

"I've had enough." Derek turned to the door.

The child seized his hand and bit down on his little finger, pinching it as hard as possible with its back teeth as if trying to split it open, the pain shooting along his arm. With a yell, Derek swung towards the cabin wall, slamming the child into the toughened cedar. His hand was burning now, a cold burn as if it was encased in ice, and a greenish foam was bubbling from the child's mouth. Derek snarled and mashed it against the wall again and again, the child gnawing all the time. On the fourth or fifth impact, its head split open along one side, and the jaw released, so that Derek's hand came free and the child slumped to the floor. The stink of rotten milk was overpowering.

There was no blood. Only a viscous, albumen-like fluid that oozed from the broken head to pool thickly on the planks. Derek stepped closer, the crook of his arm pressed over mouth and nose. The child's head was hollow. Beneath the skin, which seemed to be a thick layer of hard tissue, like the shell of an insect, there was only the fluid.

Derek looked to his hand. His pinkie was red and wrinkled and hung loosely at an odd angle. He touched it gingerly. It was entirely numb.

He stumbled from the cabin and knelt on the wet grass outside, his forehead pressed against the hard ground, trying not to pass out. It had turned colder, a tang of snow on the air. He stayed down for some time, trying to ignore the chill that worked its way into his bones, until he started to shiver, teeth banging painfully together.

Perhaps it wouldn't do to call the police after all. Derek was no longer sure he hadn't done anything wrong, or how he might explain what was in the cabin. No, he would have to sort this out himself.

Once he was sure he'd be able to walk, he slowly made his way back to Glynwood, and the lean-to where he kept his tools.

ᥫᩣ ᥫᩣ

The splinters weren't easy to remove.

Derek sat in the armchair by the fire, working at his fingers with a needle and tweezers. His toolbox stood on the floor by his feet, and his clothes still bore streaks of dirt from the clayey soil beneath the cabin. It had taken most of the afternoon to pry up the cabin's floorboards and dig a hole in the cold earth that was large enough to accommodate the child's shell-like remains and the withered body of the old woman. It would have been quite a task even for a young man. When Derek had finished it had been all he could do to get back to the house, set a fire in the grate, and sink into his chair. His toolbox was at his feet; he'd been too tired to put it away.

Once the splinters were all out, he poured himself a large measure of Glenfiddich from the bottle on the side table and stared into the flames. He still couldn't be sure what had truly occurred, nor what to do next. Selling the property might be prudent. The house had been a steal in the first place: property was dirt cheap in this part of Monmouthshire. Or he could add it to his rental portfolio and buy another grand house to retire to. He had money, and money provided options.

But what if whoever moved in got rid of the cabin and found the shallow grave beneath? Perhaps it would be better to stay and pretend it had never happened. He swallowed the whiskey and basked in the warmth it brought. There was no need for a quick decision, he decided. Time to ruminate.

He poked again at his pinkie. Some of the feeling had returned now, but the digit remained soft and wrinkled. He couldn't move it. Perhaps tomorrow he would consult a doctor, if he could come up with a good explanation for its condition.

He watched the fire once more.

A faint click made him stir, and he realised that he'd dozed. The small clock on the mantelpiece indicated it was almost one in the morning. The fire had burned low, the embers still lambent beneath a layer of ash.

Another click, this time one that he recognised. The front door closing.

Derek reached to the toolbox and took up his crowbar, twisted fragments of cedar still clinging to the edge. He watched the door to the hallway, hardly breathing.

The handle turned and a familiar face poked around the door. Large beard, broad nose, salt-and-pepper hair. Terry. The contractor raised his eyebrows.

"Mr Broome."

"Terry. What are you doing, letting yourself into my house at this hour?" Derek felt his face flush, anger prickling across his skin, the events of the day flooding back to him. "Kept your own key, eh?"

"Aye. I did." The contractor stepped into the room, dressed in overalls and carrying a leather workman's satchel, as if he'd just come from a job in the middle of the night. "Just in case."

"In case what?" Derek shifted his grip on the crowbar in his lap.

Terry spread his hands. "In case you had any trouble, Mr Broome."

Derek's mouth was dry but he daren't reach for his drink.

"What kind of trouble?"

Terry shrugged. Derek found it an oddly child-like gesture.

"Trouble settling in. Took you a while to open the cabin, then?"

"You know what was in there?"

Terry nodded. "A hungry child, needing to grow. And Mrs Aderyn Price. A local woman, from

Beili-glas. She came willingly, cross my heart. Nothing holding her to the table, was there?"

Derek gaped. "Willingly?"

"She knew how to give back, did Aderyn. That's not so common these days. Too many people grown old without learning what's owed. Old misers like you, hoarding up everything because you think you deserve it, that you've earned it through skill and hard work, rather than it falling into your lap because you happened to be born in the right place, at the right time. And the children wait for scraps."

"What was that… thing? The child."

Terry scratched at his beard. "One of a family," he said quietly. "They're the past. And the future. My old nain called 'em the bones of the earth. Take the bones away, a thing don't last very long."

"Like Mrs Aderyn Price."

Terry smiled and pulled a hammer from his satchel, letting it hang casually at his side. "I felt that child die, Mr. Broome. I don't expect you to understand. I'm not sure you can. But my own feelings change nothing.

"Now. It's easy enough, I promise you. Virtually painless. If the children starve, so does the land. So do we all. And you've had a good run, Mr. Broome. How many properties do you own? How much money do your tenants bring you every month? It's been a life to envy.

"Let's go to the garden. Please, Mr Broome."

Derek struggled to his feet, balancing the crowbar in shaking hands.

"Don't even think about it, Mr Broome." Terry stepped forward warily. "It can only end one way."

Derek lunged.

ഛഉ ഉഛ

Snow was falling, the flakes thick beneath a starless sky. Derek watched them spiral down, thousands upon thousands of them, there and gone, each one beautiful but vanished in an instant. What a terrible waste.

His back ached. The tabletop was hard. His arms and legs had been secured to the table with steel chains that pressed tight against his bare skin. Terry had been honest, at least. It had all been painless enough. The work of a moment to overpower an old man like him, truss him up and, once the farmhouse table had been brought out to the garden, set him atop it like a lamb joint waiting to be carved.

Terry stood a short distance away, gazing out over the fields, though the man could surely see very little in the moonless night. The only thing Derek could discern in the darkness was a faint speck of light, a marker of a distant house on the other side of the valley.

"Don't have any children of your own, I think, Mr Broome? An unnecessary distraction, perhaps."

Derek refused to speak. If he had to die, he would do so with dignity. Terry was right, though. Children hadn't been all that important to Derek. Fine in theory, just not in practice. He'd thought family a burden. Seemed a regrettable outlook at that moment. But perhaps it was the nature of such realisations that they should arrive too late.

"Who gets all those houses, I wonder. When you're gone. Not the people who live in them, for sure. I daresay they might find themselves looking for other homes, when—whoever, the bank I suppose—inherits and decides to sell up." He shook his head. "This place'll sell soon enough, I expect. Always plenty of rich old folks looking for cheap country houses."

Derek sensed movement around him, white figures dancing through the snowflakes. Half a dozen, at least.

"So many," he whispered, despite himself.

"It's not a punishment, Mr Broome," said Terry. "More of a... balancing. To keep them going. I'll take my turn too, one day. And gladly." He turned away as the children crept closer.

"Wait!" Derek yelled. "It doesn't have to be me. There must be others! And there are other ways I can pay it back. Please!"

The snow descended in silence.

Hours later, yet still before the dawn, they had gone. Back to the hills, Derek supposed. For now. He was almost entirely numb. Terry had left shortly after the children had started feeding, and so Derek was entirely alone. The snow no longer fell, though it lay thick upon the ground and on Derek's torso.

They'd started with his hands and feet. He couldn't see much as he lay, but his right arm was close enough to his face for him to recognise that the withered, flaccid limb was useless. Yet if he concentrated, he was sure his elbow moved when he tried to flex his shoulder.

Pushing his shoulder and elbow against the table as hard as he could—as far as he could tell, with the numbness—he dragged against the chain, and was rewarded with the sight of his collapsed limb inching free. The skin tore, sloughing off as it went, but this served to lubricate the chain further, and after a few more tries his right arm was clear of its shackle. It dangled over the side of the table.

He turned his attention to the other arm.

After that, by working at his shoulders and thighs, rocking back and forth, he managed to drag his legs loose. Each limb was ragged and ruined. But he could move his elbows and knees, and his neck.

Inch by inch, he shuffled to the edge of the table and dropped, landing face first in the snow. The scent of ice and earth filled him completely.

There was no help to be had at Glynwood. He wouldn't even be able to get through the door, and Terry was likely to return at some point, even if just to tidy away the mess.

The only chance he had was to find someone. On knee and elbow, each movement jarring his back and neck, he crawled to the edge of the garden, where a hedge of hazel and honeysuckle marked the boundary between his property and the pasture beyond. The snow was cold against his flesh, making him shiver. But that was good—the numbness was beginning to fade, perhaps.

He pushed on, through the rough, grasping hedgerow and into the field, a vast plain of blackness that dipped into the distance before rising again on the other side, where another house and another person waited. The light still burned there, a beacon in the night.

There was a long way to go before Derek could reach it. An eternity. But crawl towards the light was the only thing he could do.

FICTION

SCRATCHING

by Alys Key

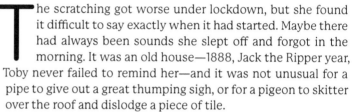

T he scratching got worse under lockdown, but she found it difficult to say exactly when it had started. Maybe there had always been sounds she slept off and forgot in the morning. It was an old house—1888, Jack the Ripper year, Toby never failed to remind her—and it was not unusual for a pipe to give out a great thumping sigh, or for a pigeon to skitter over the roof and dislodge a piece of tile.

Susie's flat was at the top of the house, just an attic above it. The scratching gave that empty space scale, pushed a gap into her mind where the worst things lived: rats, spiders, cockroaches, mice.

"You have to seal everything up Suze," Toby told her. "One time in my old house I picked up a loaf of bread and something had tunnelled right through it, like *The Great Escape*."

"Very reassuring, thanks," she said to the laptop screen. She had placed him on top of two recipe books in the kitchen and angled it so they could talk while she cooked.

"Anyway, get the landlord in."

"Letting agent says it'll be a few weeks. Pest control shortage."

He nodded in that *yes of course* way he had when she told him something he didn't know.

"They're probably all looking after offices in the City," he said. "Everyone's scared they'll come back from remote working and find families of rats in their filing cabinets."

She thought about the bookshop where they both worked, imagined it crawling with lumps of dirty fur and fat naked tails. She could see them spilling out of the shop doors and onto the cobbles of Leadenhall Market, where they would surge past the Lamb & Flag and make for the shining spires of the Cheesegrater, the Scalpel, the Gherkin.

She pushed chunks of onion into the pan and went to wash her hands.

"How's the new walk?" she shouted over the tap.

"Fantastic. Did you know how many plague pits there are around the Square Mile?"

"Strangely, no." She dried her hands a little too roughly, making the skin between her thumb and fingers smart.

"The ground is stuffed with them. And I can just tack it onto my Great Fire of London tour. It's an easy narrative to sell, you know?"

She pulled a bottle of white wine from the fridge. "Death and destruction? It's what every tourist wants." She raised a glass to him and he scowled.

"Not just that... though obviously that's part of it. I mean the narrative of a fresh start after disease. The Fire cleared the way for better buildings, better living standards. It's a turning point."

She thought about this as she plated up the curry—it was a recipe from one of the many books she had snatched before the shop was locked up and they'd all been placed on the government's payroll.

"Will we need something like that, d'you think? A great flood or fire to wash away the virus?"

"If you mean a fundamental change then I think it's already happening. Lots of things won't be the same after this."

"No," she said. "They won't."

࿐

That night the bursts of scratching came infrequently, and each time they roused her from a thinner and thinner sleep until she was just lying awake, a tight band of anticipation around her stomach. She didn't consider herself to be a wimp about these sorts of things. Living alone had given her a utilitarian confidence in her own abilities, so she was not squeamish about flipping spiders out of the window, or spraying bin-flies and collecting their lint-ball black bodies onto an envelope.

What was vile to her, in this instance, was the way the creatures—mice or rats or whatever they were—had changed their habits at the same time as humans. When she couldn't sleep she looked at articles about how vermin had lost one of their main sources of food when London's restaurants closed their doors. No more scraps and unsold stock served bleeding ripe liquid onto street corners.

It was happening all over the world. She read about a place in New York where the residents were engaged in a turf war with the rats, watched videos of them chasing the invaders into the street with brooms.

"We're more scared of the rats than we are of the virus at this point," one woman said.

She knew how she felt. All around the empty streets of East London pressed in and the shape of her own home was starting to feel changed, unfriendly. The presence on the other side made the very fabric of the ceiling different. The room was too hot and itchy.

"Go away, go away," she whispered into the dark.

Something answered with a trembling scrape and then there was silence.

࿐

She went to queue outside the big Tesco, holding the carrier bag in which she kept all her other carrier bags. She was following Toby's advice. Plastic tubs, freezer bags, masking tape, bleach, rat poison—her basket looked like a 'my first murder' kit. There was hardly any room for the food.

On her way back, people passed her on the pavement in clumsy swinging motions to keep their distance, some of them carrying oversized groceries like her, others just walking. Victoria Park had closed that week and her corner of London, a no man's land between Bethnal Green and Bow, was dazed by the loss of it. Runners and dog-walkers kept turning up in estates and on side-streets where they had never gone before.

Her road was quiet, as it usually was. The row of houses, leading to a dead end, looked much as they had 100 years ago—untouched by the Tube, the Blitz, the developers.

Behind the front door of her building was a dark corridor where post collected like dirt. She paused inside, setting down the shopping. Her hands were rubbed raw and stiff by the heavy bags. She stood stretching them for a moment, and noticed there was a piece of paper tied to the bannister.

Dear neighbours,
I am going to try clearing the garden so we can all use it while things are the way they are. Find me there 12-4 most days if you would like to help or have a socially distanced cup of tea.
Alan (Flat A)

It was her first encounter with this kind of sudden community impulse in real life, but she had seen it on Facebook. There was something irritating about it. Why was neighbourly feeling the reserve of disaster?

She left the poster and lugged her things up the two flights of creaking stairs that came onto a little landing outside her flat.

She tried not to look up once she got to this spot, but every time her eyes slid unbidden to it: a hatch in the ceiling. It was the only way to access the loft, and it was a small comfort to her that it was not inside her flat. When she stood below it, her skin prickled.

࿐

"I think you should help the old guy out Suze, he's probably lonely. And you always moan about the state of the garden."

Toby's eyes were underscored grey and looked

wet, overspilling with the white light from his screen.

"I don't like it." She scratched a couple of flakes from a dry patch just above her elbow. "It feels a bit forced."

"God," he rolled his eyes. "I bet you're one of those people who over-analyses the 'clap for carers' thing as well. People act differently in pandemics. Speaking of... do you want to hear my new stories for the tour? I found a Victorian one for you."

"Go on then," she said, emptying the bottle into her glass with a theatrical sigh.

"Right." Off-camera she could hear him unpacking his notes. "1889. There's this young doctor who moves to the East End, chasing the idea of making a medical breakthrough.

"The thing is it's almost the end of the century. Typhoid, cholera—the big ones have already been solved, so this poor doctor is a bit late to the game. But there's still syphilis, scabies, Russian flu, not to mention arsenic-tinted beer and smog and unexplained cot deaths abound."

"I thought this was a pandemic story?"

"Well it's sort of just disease, I've gone down a bit of a rabbit hole... anyway bear with me. So, he treats the poor, goes into their homes and gets close to them. Inevitably he starts catching things and has to be laid up for weeks at a time. But he always gets better and goes back into the field.

"Finally he gets something he can't diagnose. It's a skin disease. Hardly visible but he can't stop scratching. Then it makes him hallucinate. He's bleeding, he's raving, he's in a terrible way. Other tenants in his building complain about the screaming. Finally it gets too much for the landlady and she goes upstairs."

He paused, letting Susie become aware of how neatly he had looped her into this story and was now pulling the thread tight. It annoyed her; how good he was at this.

"As she opens the door she sees him, calm as you like, sitting at his desk with his surgical tools out. Then she notices that the copy of *The Times* laid out neatly under his elbows is drenched with blood. She comes closer and he turns to look at her. That's when she sees his left hand sat on the desk, cut clean off at the wrist.

"The landlady goes screaming from his room and her two big sons run up and grab him before he can cut off the other one.

"They bandage him up and get another doctor to look at him, but for hours they have to sit in the room with him and hold his good arm to stop him gnawing at his wrist. When they ask him why he would do such a thing, he says: 'it was the only way I could stop the scratching.'"

They sat in a grim silence.

"How do you always manage to find the worst stories?"

"It's a gift." He grinned, but it stretched into a yawn. "That's the gist of that one."

"What happened to him?"

"I don't know. The only other detail I could find from these penny dreadful news reports was that he had got himself a prosthetic hand."

"I didn't know Victorians had prosthetics."

"Oh yeah, they're creepy though. It's either elaborate steampunk-type stuff with long metal fingers, or just rotting wood with a hook in the palm."

"Hmm." Susie and Toby had based their friendship on a shared fascination with the macabre. Her dissertation, on Victorian ghost stories, had furnished him with several details for his walking tours. But now she wasn't in the mood. It seemed a cheap kind of darkness. "Can we talk about something else?"

"Shall we just call it a night? You look tired."

"I don't really feel like sleeping yet." She glanced at the ceiling, willed the sounds to start up again, loud enough for Toby to hear. She wanted him to confirm their sickly quality, to see her own shudder mirrored in his shoulders.

"Come on," he said. "I'm sleepy."

She let him go, but stayed up a while longer flicking through YouTube. Nothing stuck. Before lockdown, her attention span had allowed her to read multiple books a day, whole classics and Booker winners, down the hatch in time for dinner. Now it was betraying her.

She shut off the laptop and got ready for bed with a cold resignation. When she climbed in, she held a pillow over the back of her head.

She was sure the hairs on her neck stood up half a second before the first scraping began, and then there was a quick rush of tapping, like someone drumming their fingers on a table.

⁂

She spent the next few days cleaning.

There were stacks of books in the fireplace—proofs and damaged copies salvaged from work. A few weeks earlier, she had posted a picture of them, tagged it #lockdownreads and been pleased with how the evening light illuminated her little flat. Now all she saw was a warren of hiding places. She couldn't donate the books so she found space on the shelves, wedging them between her battered copies of Le Fanu and Wilkie Collins.

She vacuumed and wiped down surfaces, changed the bedclothes, threw out old birthday cards, receipts and magazines. When she was done her hands were pruned and raw. She smoothed on some lotion but still they stung with a pink heat she couldn't shift. The only relief came from washing the lotion off again and rough-drying her hands until the skin was flecked with small openings where blood rose to the surface.

The irritation lasted for days. And it spread. Her hours became disordered, lacerated with periods in which she did nothing except lie still on the sofa, trying not to scratch, until she relented and scraped her nails across her ribs or the backs of her thighs or her neck. Relieving that rough gnaw was ecstatic, a guilty thrill running all the way through her that left her punch-drunk for a few moments before the pain set in. Later, the itching would return.

She didn't know what day it was when she went out into the garden. It had been another sleepless night and she was starting to feel emptied out. She floated through her morning without noticing it, and then at midday she was downstairs, a coffee in hand, stepping outside.

Alan from Flat A was bent over in a thicket of bindweed and crisp packets. She cleared her throat and he turned to face her.

"Oh, good morning."

"Hi... Alan? I'm Susie, I live on the top floor?"

"Yes of course, delightful to see you." He started taking off his gardening gloves then stopped. "Ah, I suppose no handshakes."

"I suppose not," she said. "I thought I could help you out."

"Excellent!" He beamed. He had a round face, looked mid-to-late 60s. He seemed like the kind of person who wore bow ties with fun patterns on them to special occasions—back when there had been special occasions to go to.

"Well," he said. "Have you got a pair of gardening gloves?"

"No, sorry."

"Not to worry. I've some spares. They might be a touch too big, mind."

He looked at her hands, sizing them up, and she realised he would be able to see the flaking patches and the track marks left by her nails. She tugged her sleeves lower.

But he was already pulling things from his toolbox and laying them out: a few trowels, some weed killer, a long set of hedge shears. He produced the gloves.

"So," he said, handing them to her. "How do you get on with rakes?"

The garden was a disaster. Over the years it had filled with bits of brick, litter, a bike wheel with most of its spokes missing, plant pots, and all sorts of other junk. Weedy tendrils crawled into every available space and sometimes crawled back again over the top, making a thick tapestry of foliage. Alan pointed out different plants as they found them. Japanese knotweed, Herb Robert, chickweed, crabgrass.

By the end of the afternoon they had cleared a small section close to the house. It did not look pretty, a rough bit of earth holding out against the raging plants threatening at any moment to invade it.

Alan fetched two folding metal chairs from inside, which he set up in their new clearing. He darted back in and came out with two wineglasses and a bottle of Pinot Grigio. They sat in the chairs drinking, and looked at what they had yet to tame.

"I take it you're not one of these people who can work from home then? Nothing better to do than help an old man in his hopeless project?"

"I'm on furlough. I work at a bookshop in the City." She sipped the wine. It was good stuff, floral, warming her tongue and cheeks as she watched the sunlight turn gold. "What about you?"

"Retired now, but I do bits and pieces. I worked in theatre, so I doubt there'll be much of that for a long time."

"No."

"Never mind. Plenty of reading time for you I suppose?"

She swallowed another mouthful of wine, weighed up what to say. In normal circumstances, she would be scared to look unhinged in front of her neighbour. But Toby was right, the rules were different in pandemics.

"I've been a bit distracted to be honest. Not sleeping too well."

"Mind racing? Mine does that if I read the news."

"That's it, sometimes. But there's also this… noise I keep hearing above me. In the attic. I guess it's just mice or something but it's really unsettled me."

He nodded. "Doesn't surprise me in this house."

"You've heard it too?"

"Not that specifically, but this building… I went to look up the address at the records office once and found out that in 1918, every single resident of this house died of Spanish Flu."

"What?!"

"Just—" he clicked his fingers a few times "— one after the other, like that."

He shivered with a touch of drama and she began to wonder if he was telling the truth.

Just then, there was a movement in the still-wild garden. Something was pushing through the long grasses.

"There she is," Alan said. His voice dissolved into a series of coos and kissing noises as the shape emerged. It was a cat.

It butted against Alan's outstretched hand until he started scratching behind its ears. It was black and white and solid in a way that Susie liked, not overfed but not too thin.

"This is my darling girl Bush," said Alan. "Named after Kate, of course."

Susie nodded and eyed the cat's little snarl of tooth, the prick of claw poking from her marshmallow paws. An idea struck her.

"I don't suppose I could borrow her for a moment?"

The three of them made an odd procession, Susie leading the way upstairs while Alan trailed at a distance and stopped every few steps to leave Dreamies on the carpet. Bush brought up the rear, picking off the treats as she went.

When they came to the landing, Alan looked around and said, "This isn't a bad space you know, you could claim it since you're the only one up here, add a desk and chair."

Susie made a vague noise of agreement, even

though the thought of sitting out here with her back to the hatch in the ceiling made a terrible crawling run from the back of her neck right down to her tailbone.

"Come on," Alan was saying to the cat, still a few steps behind. "Come on Mrs, come and check Miss Susie's flat for her, hmmm?"

But Bush was unresponsive. She sat down and stared, then slowly lifted her face until her gold-rimmed eyes were fixed on the ceiling. A whining started. It sounded at first like it was coming from all around them, a discordant hum filtering up through the walls. Then the hiss overlaid it and Susie realised it was the cat, baring her teeth, spine curled and tense.

"Bushy stop that." Alan put another treat on the top step but Bush only backed further away. "Sorry about this," he said. "Never seen her so on-edge."

Susie's neck started to itch. Once she noticed it, she felt the same clawed tingle on her hands and hips and shoulders.

"That's OK, you'd better take her back downstairs. I'll see you tomorrow, in the garden?"

She rushed into her flat, closed the door, and began scratching furiously under her clothes. Bits of skin flaked off and clumped under her nails. In the attic, the dreadful scrabbling sounds echoed the rhythmic tearing.

She was in the shower when she decided to cut her own hair. She was in a mood for throwing things away.

She had spent the afternoon in the garden with Alan's giant set of shears. The blades, slicing so decisively through the overgrowth, had made easy gashes in the weeds. Once cut, she could pull the plants apart with the rake, like she was combing a giant's unruly hair. And when that was done, she had grabbed clumps with her gloved hands and shoved them into binbags.

The water started to run cold. She had developed a bad habit lately of turning the heat up and up until she was being lashed with almost-scalding water that burned away the itching. It did have the downside of exhausting her boiler's abilities, and she stepped out of the shower shivering, her skin aching in the evening air.

There was a big pair of scissors in the kitchen drawer, something that had already been in the flat when she moved in. They looked old, but the heavy steel cut through her hair with a fresh sharpness. She stood in front of the mirror above the fireplace, still wearing a towel, and started to trim.

❦

"Looks good," Toby told her through a mouthful of lasagne that evening as she angled her head for the webcam.

"I'm not sure I've done it right at the back."

"Well, get it fixed in a few weeks and nobody will see it in the meantime."

"I hope it is a few weeks."

"Me too. Did I tell you I think I've got enough for two pandemic tours now? One about 1665 and one about disease through the ages."

"How are you going to have time for all these?"

"Dunno. If it takes off I might quit the shop."

"I'd be sad if you did," she said, though she couldn't even imagine the shop anymore. Unpacking boxes, helping someone find the Bear Grylls books (very popular with City types), taking cash from a customer's hand and smiling, it all seemed absurd. Like ghosts caught in a moment of history, uselessly carrying out the same things they did before.

❦

The scratching was no longer confined to night-time. It put her off her breakfast and pierced through whatever music she put on to drown it out.

Sleep became a tawdry thing. She was so tired it made being awake a dream, and when she was in bed her mind made shapes and picked holes in reality. Every morning she had to open Twitter and submit to half an hour of doomscrolling, just to establish which things were true and which she had made up to scare herself.

Her skin was getting worse.

There came a night when something in her crumbled. She heard noises and saw things moving. All her books were falling off their shelves and her flat was filling with them. She had to get out or face a paper drowning.

She only had to think of the garden and then she was there, gargling the grass as she crawled through it, chasing a moonlight gleam poking out of the toolbox. Then it was in her hand. The han-

dles of the hedge shears felt so plastic-smooth, almost obscene against the hungry edge of the blade.

It was solid to the touch but she was not solid herself. She had been worn down and her mind was empty of everything but the scratching. To do it would be easy, the cutting free of Peter Pan's shadow.

Still lying on the untamed lawn, she opened the jaws of the shears, fed her arm into it, and then time went blackly raw.

❦

It was Alan who had found her. Afterwards he would not stop apologising for breaking social distancing to tear her away, even though she would have cut open her veins and bled out onto the grass without his intervention. Or torn off her own hand.

Toby, too, was in a guilty mood.

"I'm sorry Suze, I should have realised you weren't coping and shut up with my stupid stories."

He had come to collect her. After Alan bundled her into his flat and called the paramedics, who concluded she only had minor scratches, it had been decided that she would go and live with Toby.

"It's not your fault. I haven't been dealing with my own issues," she said. "Not to be pathetic but could you go upstairs and grab me some clothes? I can't... I find it hard to go up there."

He agreed and left Alan's flat, but returned only a few seconds later.

"He's only finally arrived."

"Who has?"

"Pest control."

The man was in full Ghostbuster kit, boiler suit and some kind of silver tank on his back. He held a toolbox in one hand.

"Miss Smith? Sorry about the delay. Heard you've been having problems with the attic."

He went up with Toby while she remained in the corridor long enough to hear the clank of the hatch being opened, the metal ladder slithering out. It made her feel sick.

She went out to the garden and found Alan hard at work, while Bush stretched out with her belly facing the sun. She lay down next to the cat.

She woke up with that salty afternoon nap taste on her tongue and a chill creeping into her skin. The sun had gone behind a cloud.

Toby was just coming outside with the pest control man, who was holding a thick plastic bag.

"What is that?" she asked, visions of rodent bodies stacking up in her brain.

"It's good news," said the man. "I couldn't find any traces of vermin in the attic, or in your flat."

He might as well have told her she had been living in a building made of water, it was so contrary to what she understood to be true. She looked at Toby, who looked even guiltier than before, and on top of that, a dry-mouthed kind of pale. He wouldn't meet her eye.

"I did find this." The man held out the bag. She half-expected it to be oozing blood but she took it anyway, resolved to sing two, maybe three, Happy Birthdays when she washed her hands later.

"Suze," Toby started. "Maybe you shouldn't..."

But it was too late. She had looked inside and seen it: a rusted conglomeration of metal pieces that, together, formed the ghoulish outline of a human hand.

⋰⊙⊙⋱

Tower Hamlets Cemetery is one of the magnificent seven cemeteries of London, opened between 1833 and 1841. Toby had been to all of them.

"Definitely one of the best," he was saying. "This one, Abney Park and Nunhead are like my holy trinity of lush woodland graveyards. Highgate's just full of people taking selfies with Marx."

Susie knew he was only talking so much because she was tired and silent. Since moving into his spare room a few days earlier, she had finally slept again. She loved the pink-blue light that punched through the thin curtains early in the morning, and she loved ignoring it to roll over into more sleep.

Still, she was exhausted. Stress buzzed through her all the time, made her feel low and weak no matter how much she rested. The trip to the cemetery had been Toby's suggestion. He thought it might be a kind of remedy, to find the grave and lay to rest what was troubling her.

Knowing the doctor's address had made it easier to find out more about him. He had died young, at just 30-years-old, never married. He had been buried in the cemetery's eastern half but they were not sure where exactly.

It really was a woodland. Shaded all over by layers of leaves that shuffled across each other with the smoothness of playing cards. There were more paths than the map could show, dust trails leading to graves that slumped into the ground under handfuls of moss and wildflowers. They were everywhere, these little slabs of name and number. Every available patch of earth had been filled and then filled again.

"We'll never find him," she said, surprised to find herself disappointed.

"We will."

They each took a row at a time and met up again when the paths crossed to report their findings. There were sea captains and soldiers, social reformers, music hall singers. There were grand family vaults with bits missing.

The flowers in Susie's hand were wilting when she heard Toby call her name. He was up a little slope, standing by a grave no higher than his shin.

Dr. Alfred Willis
9th July 1862—5th October 1892

That was all it said. There was no enigmatic stanza of poetry, no ghoulish engraving of a skull or mysterious symbol.

"That's it?"

"Yep," said Toby. "One-handed Alfie." She gave him a look. "Sorry."

Susie placed the little bouquet on the ground, tried to spruce up the lavender stems and adjust the ribbon so it looked presentable.

"There." It looked a paltry offering, but it matched the paltry headstone. "Well... rest easy doctor."

Toby patted the stone, and they made their way back down the slope together in silence.

Outside the cemetery bounds, she exhaled.

"Feeling any better?" he asked.

"Yeah. I still don't know if I believe it was that... thing." She tried not to think about the rusting metal joints of the fingers, the slender point of the thumb. It was in the Science Museum now, safely on the other side of the city. Toby had taken care of that. "But I think it helped."

Toby put his arm around her shoulders and they smiled at each other. With his other hand, he reached up and scratched a spot on his neck, where a sudden itching had just begun.

FICTION

EYES LIKE PISTILS

by Evan James Sheldon

When Clive meets the priest he's desperate, living in the woods, and wandering on and on. He's made mistakes, sure. The kind of mistakes that accumulate, the kind that branch off one another until you don't even remember the road leading here. He's not even sure where these particular woods belong. Oregon? Washington? He got lost trying to find a commune where they grew things that, when consumed, pulled back the veil covering this world, things that helped you forget even as your mind expanded. He seeks a gentle transformation.

It is dark but the moon is out so the wavering leaves and branches look silver and magic. He watches the priest approach but is too worn down to run, to do anything other than wait, his hunger momentarily forgotten. They are deep in the trees and far from civilization.

Once he draws near, the priest himself doesn't look right, somehow misshapen in the moonlight. He smells of honey and sunlight, wild grass and forest mold; a nice smell even if he doesn't look nice. He holds out two globular seeds. We, as believers, should never pass up an opportunity for forgiveness. The priest is a big man, bigger than seems reasonable, bigger than men should be. His skin jumps and twitches, transitorily bulbous then slack, like he is filled with multitudes.

Clive swallows one seed dry, a skill from his not-so-distant past. It slides down easy, with purpose, and almost immediately he feels it anchor in his belly. The priest smiles, a horrible and lovely sight, and doesn't partake. He presses the other seed into Clive's open, trembling hand. Bury this. I'll be back in a week. You will be different then. You will be sanctified. Prepare for my return. He doesn't explain and he walks off into the woods.

Clive doesn't move for a long time, remembering what it was like when he was the one wearing vestments, when he was the one doling out forgiveness. It seems like a long time ago, and maybe it was. He prays for relief, for a new beginning, and when he breaks through the trees, across a wide grassy field, he finds the house waiting for him.

⚬⚬ ⚬⚬

He intends to knock, to see if whoever lives in the house has any work he can do in exchange for some food, some rest. He isn't the type to freeload, to expect something in return for nothing, but when no one answers, he surprises himself and enters.

The place is filled with all sorts of junk—yellow piles of the local post, eight different old-timey record players in various sizes, dirty clothes and rugs thrown over more piles offering up strange hidden creatures pretending to be ghosts. Food wrappers and cigarette butts and plastic toys and empty green bottles, and more and more. There must be thousands of batteries. Clive understands the sentiment. Emptiness can gnaw at a person. Sometimes it is better to fill a space, even with meaningless things.

He smells the body right away. If you've smelled one corpse you won't ever mistake the scent for anything else. But even still, it takes Clive a while to find the old man on the kitchen floor. A hundred or so empty pill bottles edge the counter with dates going back several years. Clive doesn't recognize the medication but guesses it's for a heart or a liver or whatever other fragile bits that come together to make a person. He doesn't like medications. If God has punched your ticket, who are you to fight against divine mandate? Little capsules won't do anything to prevent the failings of someone's interior. Plus, pills clutch with the strongest hands, hold on most fiercely. Still, he licks a finger and runs it around a couple of the empty bottles. The dust tastes chalky and bitter, and he salivates, remembering.

Even though the house sits in the middle of nowhere, he doesn't want to take any chances. So once it is dark, he wraps the body in a stained Little Shop of Horrors comforter and drags it outside. The ground by the porch is tough, but he wants to give the old man his due. He buries the old man, shallow but covered; obligation and need can be the same thing.

⚬⚬ ⚬⚬

The next day Clive plants the seed next to the old man. It is the same in every way to the one the priest gave him in the woods. As much as he's curious about what it will grow into, this holy plant, a small part of him hopes that it won't grow into anything at all. No shoots. No buds. No strangling vines strong enough to slowly crack concrete. Just a regular seed in the dead ground with no consequence.

He also knows he has to keep it alive, if only to see what it will become. He lights a cigarette—

not his brand—and it tastes wrong on his tongue, almost sweet, and he blows smoke over where he has planted the seed. He imagines himself as the seed, peering up through rocky bits of soil and smoke to see his own face hovering above like a ruined sun.

That evening it begins to rain—not a drizzle or even a steady spatter, but a late summer flash flood. Water gushes off the corner of the roof, gutters overrun. Clive looks around for something, anything, and finds an upturned frisbee he's been using as an ashtray. Rushing over to the edge of the concrete, he holds the frisbee over the buried seed. Cold water runs off his jaw, down his back, he can barely see through the deluge, but he keeps the frisbee steady. The priest was right; the barest of sprouts has pushed up through the dirt already. It's green, he's sure of it, but it looks black in the storm.

He can feel the same plant growing inside him, it's small now, but unmistakable. He must know the shape of it as it fills him. To know its shape would be a map of his soul, an outline of his interior. He'll keep them alive, the one in his gut and the one in the dirt, until he knows. Before he even begins to tire, the rain gentles, a small mercy.

⁓ം⊛ ⊛ം⁓

Clive wonders how he knew the man in the woods was a priest. Like recognizes like, perhaps. Maybe it was something about how he approached, his gait light like he wanted to touch the earth gently, already floating toward the heavens. Even still, Clive is very aware that he and the priest in the woods are different. Different in appearance, yes, but also on a deeper level, as if they are composed of unlike materials. He sees himself in the priest, and while that would normally bring a measure of empathy, and it does, he also is afraid. He doesn't know what that fear means. Now that he has rested, the whole experience takes on a surreal light, shadows appearing where they shouldn't exist, stretched too far, moonlight glinting where it shouldn't, memory exaggerating truth into the beginnings of terror.

⁓ം⊛ ⊛ം⁓

The plant grows more each day, sprouting delicate tendrils from an ever-thickening trunk. It is beautiful, in its way, dark and intricate, as if made of lace and shadow. Its leaves are soft to the touch, spread wide on firm stems.

Clive feels the same plant, an exact mirror, growing inside him. His belly is full with it and if he moves in just the right way, he can feel the softness of the leaves brush against his insides. It is a gift.

He's been hungry for so long and now he is continually satisfied. He doesn't eat. He opens his mouth wide, head tilted back toward the sun. He drinks just enough water to give the sprout what it needs without drowning it. He worries though, if the plant in the ground should wither, so might the one growing inside him.

All good things require work. So he lingers over the plant, like a wise farmer, like a good father. He tries to smoke less.

⁓ം⊛ ⊛ം⁓

When Clive's not tending to his plants, he searches the house. At first, he doesn't want to disturb the old man's things, but quickly he comes to think of it as his inheritance. All grace is, by definition, a gift, and the hoarded junk, instead of trash, becomes imbued with personal devotion. He finds as many trinkets as he can and imagines himself a life where he might have had them, along with the people to give them; perhaps a continuation of the life he abandoned. He tries on clothes, hats, gloves, and he replaces his old life, blurry with hungers of all types, with this new piecemeal fantasy.

It is easy to replace the most recent of his experiences, filled with wandering and haze; a quiet, if sometimes violent, drifting life. A life he wasn't ready for. That the priest in the woods also sneaked up on him is not lost on Clive.

⁓ം⊛ ⊛ം⁓

On the third day, the plant outside blooms. Vibrant, deep purple petals unfurl slowly like an eye-socket bruise. Their edges are uneven as if they have been torn from something larger. Jaundiced pistils dot the center of each—eyes in the darkness. They are beautiful and terrible. That's how he knows they are from heaven. When angels come down to earth, the first thing they always say is do not be afraid. Though he has never seen an angel, he can imagine that if they use a disclaimer, they must be terrifying. Looking at the blooms, he knows what it is to see something not meant for this world. They don't vibrate, not if he stares directly at them, but they seem to writhe when in the corners of his vision. Since there is no angel around to do it for him, he tells himself, do not be afraid, do not be afraid, do not be afraid.

৵৽৽ ৽৽৽

The plant quickly becomes almost humanoid in shape. Clive wonders if it is feeding on the old man's body much as the one inside him is feeding on his own flesh.

It's hot out, but he's wearing a wool suit jacket, patched at the elbows, that he found in the dead man's closet. He always imagined himself as a philosopher, a truth-seeker of things beyond human scope, and somehow the simple jacket embodies that for him, takes him a step closer to how he envisions himself to be. It is loose on him, but he doesn't know if that's a result of what's happening or simply because of a natural difference between his and the old man's physiology. It doesn't really matter, he likes it and, anyway, all things of this world will eventually be cast off.

When he first guessed the plant was feeding on him, he was overjoyed. Cleansing him, consuming his sin, and the hollowness that followed must have been a version of holiness. His mother loved to tell him cleanliness and holiness were two strands of the same strong rope. He never believed her until now; now that he can feel it.

The plant shifts in the wind, mirroring his movements, and even though he is grateful for what is happening, he can't look at it anymore. It is too near now, a malformed imitation of what it will become. He begins to smoke in the kitchen, his back to the window.

৵৽৽ ৽৽৽

To prepare for the priest, Clive begins taking everything out of the house. He carries out what he can, piling smaller items into larger vessels; crystal wine glasses all dumped into a rusted washing machine, dozens of reading glasses, some with the tags still on, into an ancient wooden bassinet. In his depleted state it takes him hours and hours, and he's running out of time.

He knows it takes longer than it should, as he spends too long peering down his gullet in the dirty bathroom mirror. He can see the plant now

pushing up his esophagus, petals nearly indistinguishable from his inner flesh, but the pistils can't be mistaken for anything other than what they are.

৵৽৽ ৽৽৽

When Clive was a priest, he'd known it all. Could quote scripture for every occasion. Held his salvation tightly in both hands. He'd comforted widows, helped the poor, done everything in his power to be humble, to see the world through the eyes of God. But then he had witnessed a miracle.

The boy had been playing in a shallow creek. Some people thought it more wild, more miraculous, he'd drowned in six inches of water than when, an hour later, he'd spewed brackish water and algae and muck all over the cold hospital bedroom, eyes fluttering open.

Clive had been there, arm around the boy's mother, already whispering of better places, gentle suns, and grace, when the boy had returned. The mother threw Clive's arm off and raced to the boy's side. It should have been a moment for celebration, of praise and thanksgiving, something to strengthen what was already strong in Clive. But what he saw in the boy's eyes at the moment of return wasn't elation, they didn't still carry the ecstatic vision of beyond. Clive only saw a vacancy, a dusky hollow that should have been filled with fire.

When he left the hospital room, no one noticed. When he left the clergy three months later, no one argued.

৵৽৽ ৽৽৽

On the sixth night, Clive starts the fire. He hasn't been able to get everything out of the house in time for it to be clean and empty, and it must be clean and empty when the priest arrives. He must be prepared. One rank of angels, the Seraphim, are said to burn with the holiness of God, the name translating to burning ones. Clive believes that the priest will know this, will understand.

He cries when he lights it, thinking of all it could have been, thinking of the life he could have made and how by morning, it will all be ash. For some reason he feels the most regret in burning the record players; their transformative power now lost, the possibility of song devoured. But holiness always comes at a cost, you must be willing to give it all up. And to his surprise, he is willing.

He doesn't worry about the plant growing just off the concrete porch. He can't. He can barely move. He lies down next to it even though it is too near the flames. The petals are in his throat and the back of his mouth, tickling his epiglottis. It's hard to breathe, let alone smoke, but he manages. One tendril splits his lips, and he bites down in spite of himself, nearly retching from the acrid fluid that leaks onto his tongue. Still, he is at peace; it will all be over soon.

⚬ᖶ⚬ ᖶ⚬

He doesn't remember falling asleep but he must have as the sun is threatening to burst through the tall grasses and trees. Clive can't move. Stems and vines and leaves have pushed outward through his skin and buried themselves into the dirt. It hurts but not more than he can bear. The dark purple petals growing from his mouth obscure much of his view, but he can see the house is still burning when the priest arrives.

Small things skitter over the priest's torn skin, which has sloughed off in places, revealing a churning mass of tiny legs and mandibles and wings. He's holding a bag, which he sets down on the grass next to Clive. Dozens and dozens of seeds spill out.

Do not be afraid, the priest says, his voice the buzz of a thousand crawling and flying things. They squirm beneath the priest's skin, which in the dawning light, Clive can see is nothing but a sheath, a necessary husk.

The insects begin to gush out of every tear, every hole, and pour over Clive. They seek the softest parts of him, orifices and membranes, thin barriers between his organs and the forest air.

As they fill him, more flood over the plant next to him. For an instant, he sees himself, or the shape of himself, and then almost in unison, the pollinators crawl or fly away, carrying his image out into the world. In that moment, he knows he was wrong; holiness is not a void but a fullness.

He also knows he will pick up the spilled bag of seeds, he will become a priest again, though one he wouldn't have recognized, the cultivator of future fields brimming with dark plants, waving in the wind and growing in size until their gentle leaves blot out the sun. As his thoughts fade, or least cease to be his own, he feels his body begin to rise, filled and born anew.

BACK ON OUR BULLSHIT

Wingspan of Severed Hands - Joanna Koch

An invisible threat lures those who oppose its otherworldly violence to become acolytes of a nameless cult. As a teenage girl struggles for autonomy, a female weapons director in a secret research facility develops a living neuro-cognitive device that explodes into self-awareness. Time is the winning predator, and every moment' spirals deeper into the heart of the beast.

Seventeen Names for Skin - Roland Blackburn

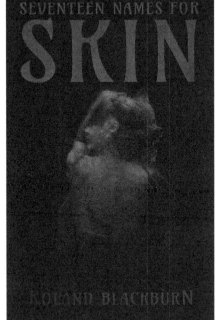

After a cancer diagnosis gives her six months to live, Snow Turner does what any introverted body-piercer might: hire a dark-web assassin and take out a massive life insurance policy to benefit her ailing father. But when a vicious attack leaves her all too alive and with a polymorphic curse, the bodies begin stacking up.

Sabbath of the Fox-Devils - Sam Richard

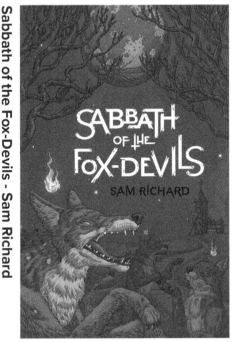

Part homage to the small-creature horror films of the 80s (Ghoulies, Gremlins, The Gate) and part Splatterpunk take on a Goosebumps book, Sabbath of the Fox-Devils is a weird, diabolical coming-of-age horror story of self-liberation in an oppressive religious environment set during the Satanic Panic.

The Mud Ballad - Jo Quenell

In a dying railroad town, a conjoined twin wallows in purgatory for the murder of his brother. A disgraced surgeon goes to desperate ends to reconnect with his lost love. When redemption comes with a dash of black magic, the two enter a world of talking corpses, flesh-eating hogs, rude mimes, and ritualistic violence.

Publishing weird horror and the grotesque since 2015.

weirdpunkbooks.com

FICTION

THE DREADFUL AND SPECIFIC MONSTER OF STAROSIBIRSK

by Kristina Ten

I know what you will say. You will say to me, Arseny, there are enough real monsters in this world—why do you make your own? But before I begin, before you make your judgments, like the others, before you *tsk-tsk-tsk* our failures and tell me what *you* would have done, there are some things that you should know.

You should know, first, that things were very bad in Starosibirsk.

You should know, also: We were once a small village of simple people on a wide, calm river. Not less, not more. We could spell the first name, father's name, and surname of everyone we knew. The homes and church and the shed for storing forest berries, we all built ourselves from strong larch wood.

The river came from the north and brought clear, cold water and many fish, among them an uncommon sturgeon known for the saltiness of its eggs. The people of Starosibirsk knew not to catch this sturgeon, nor eat its eggs, as doing so would bring a lifetime of bad luck upon the village. We heard the warning songs as children, learned to recognize it quickly and cast our lines elsewhere.

The same was not true for others in the region. For them, this caviar was beaded gold. Okay, it was not like the Ossetra you get in the western cities. But at their local markets, ten tins sold for more than a berry forager could earn in a season. So people traveled from great distances to fish in our river and eat in our cafes, to sleep in the modest guesthouses we had erected for them, or lie sleepless, fantasizing about their wealth.

The sturgeon was longer than a man and fat around the middle. On the shore, proud rybakov posed for photographs with their prizes before carrying them away. It was understood that the sturgeon was not to be slaughtered within Sta-rosibirsk limits. In their own villages—or, in times of impatience, just outside ours—they hacked dull knives through the pale bellies and harvested the eggs inside.

Returning fishermen visiting our tavern spoke freely, so we knew: Each fish contained millions of brown-black eggs in a mass so dense, they came up in whole slabs without crumbling. Fishermen lifted handfuls over their heads and hurrahed, saying "Here is Pavel's university education!" and "Here is Masha's extravagant wedding in the Balkans!" Later, they dragged the gutted fish to their kitchens on plastic sleds to be made into soup.

Then everything changed.

The accident at the nickel factory in Raboto-grad. It took only a broken pipe, a careless eye. The chemical waste leaked downstream and turned the length of the river a muddy red, the color of blood in American monster movies.

The followers of the church were the first to respond—they fell to their knees at the river of blood and covered their eyes and wept and prayed. It took the rest of us more time to understand our misfortune. We waited three weeks for the river to run clear. By then, the fish were open-mouthed and drifting. The undersides of the sturgeon were a sour yellow and rotated to face the sun.

It smelled like death, and it was. There was no debate: the eggs would not be good to eat.

For weeks after the accident, people came to see our section of the devil-touched river. Once it ran clear, they came no more.

The fish population did not recover, and those who had once traveled for the sturgeon stopped coming as well. Our guesthouses and cafes stood empty, and our tavern became among villagers the most popular place to be. Even the Starosi-birsk train station closed for lack of interest, and

we knew that there was no hope for us then.

What was left for us to believe? We had obeyed the warnings—we had not touched the sturgeon. And still bad luck had found us where we slept in our cottages, surrounded by purple berries in the summers and otherwise in snow, and it behaved as any monster would. It was thorough and unjust.

Here is another thing you should know: we were very desperate.

And also this: we were very drunk.

Finally: It was Mikhail's idea, and do not let him tell you differently. That would be classic Mikhail. When it happened, it was, "I am Mikhail, prince of the good ideas, deserving of all the credit, tell them Mikhail did it." And now it is, "I am a humble man, it was a group effort, I was merely an observer, I was only taking notes."

It happened at the tavern, six months after the accident. A night of cheap vodka and not enough zakuski to line our stomachs against the drunkenness toward which we marched. Borya and Dima fought over the little pickles and the herring on toast, while Dima's beloved mutt, the undersized borzoi, laid at his feet, waiting for scraps. Yuri, the gentleman, poured drinks and passed them around, and Maksim and I did our best to win the favor of glorious Varvara, who sat at a table nearby. And Mikhail, as you know, he came up with the idea.

Recalling our time as classmates in the physics program at Novgorod, we decided to approach the matter in a scientific way. Previously, we had approached it in a number of unscientific ways, based primarily in rage and despair and the pounding of glasses on tables.

The scientific approach was as follows:

Our observation: No one was coming to Starosibirsk, because there was no reason to come. No one was booking rooms in our guesthouses, or purchasing mushroom-stuffed piroshki or refreshing beet salads or kotleti fried to a golden brown.

Our question: What would it take for people to come to Starosibirsk, a small village no different from any other, save for its location on the river, which was now too toxic to fish or swim in, and perhaps too toxic even to sunbathe beside?

Our hypothesis: If Starosibirsk had something that no other village had, as it once did with the river sturgeon, people would come again. We agreed unanimously that, certainly, they would. And life would return to the way it was.

It would have to be quick. It would have to be compatible with our stubborn, unproductive land.

Now, Mikhail's idea.

The monster.

From the movies we watched on the tavern's old television, we knew people everywhere had a love of monsters. The experience of fear without the loss of control. The experiment of courage with the option to retreat to safety. Beautiful Hollywood actors running in the dark.

Or did meeting evil in this way convince us that we were better than we were? If a fierce creature with fanged teeth waited in the shadows, it meant little when we were rude to strangers. Cheap with our neighbors. Dishonest to our wives. Silly things in comparison.

The challenge was not only to create a dreadful monster, but one that people had not heard of before—one specific to Starosibirsk, and worth coming to see.

On a napkin between us, we drew monstrous bodies, but found it difficult to forget those we already knew. Ugly animal heads on frail human forms. A mountain monster with spiraling horns and stiff brown fur. A forest monster with arms made of branches and hands made of leaves. We were so discouraged by our lack of imagination, we almost put a stop to it then.

Then glorious Varvara shouted over from her table: "Zdravstvuyte, duraki! It is not as difficult as you make it. Think about what *you* are afraid of. In your lives. Today."

She pulled her chair over to us and called for others to join. Soon, everyone in the tavern was shouting ideas while Yuri, with the steadiest hand, poured continuous servings of vodka, and Mikhail and I, with the neatest writing, used napkins to take down notes. As soon as we filled one napkin, another appeared before us. Some were half-wet with drink and others torn and crumpled. Others were orange with grease and we, writing manically, filled them all.

"Death!" someone yelled from the back, to a room full of nods.

"Dying alone!" the bartender contributed.

"Dying poor!" said someone I could not see.

"Bears!" "Drowning!" "Ticks!" "Failure!" "Wild boars!" "Senselessness!" "My mother-in-law when she is in a bad mood!"

"Chaos," one said.

"Children," echoed another.

"Dentistry without anesthesia." A groan

moved through the tavern.

"Being trapped in the banya and overheating to death." A quiet admission from the corner, met by laughter at the unlikelihood of this.

"And you?" I asked Yuri as he refilled my glass, taking care not to spill on the notes. "What are you afraid of?"

He contemplated the bottle, then set it down and sighed. "Arseny Sergeevich." His eyes turned toward the river. "My greatest worry is that what has already happened will not be the worst that can."

We worked until the early morning, drinking steadily and combining our fears, rearranging them until they fit into one body, one history, one set of behaviors.

When the sun rose over the church's onion domes, we had a monster we could call our own.

Our monster stole the axes of woodcutters and threw the blades into the river and the shafts into the treetops where they would never be found. It lured its victims into groves and tickled them to death, or held their heads underwater and pulled out their teeth one by one. In its human form, our monster wore its shoes backwards and carried a staff, and its belly was yellow and engorged with eggs and blood. In its beast form, it had tusks protruding from both corners of its mouth and eyes the color of toxic runoff.

If you encountered our monster in the forest, you would be instructed to turn your clothing inside out, wear your shoes on opposite feet, and beg until your throat grew raw. If the monster was appeased, it would let you go free. If not, ah—you have seen the movies.

Our monster was constructed from parts of all of us. In that way, what Mikhail says about it being a group effort, a collaborative process, he is telling the truth. The next part required contributions from everyone, too.

Because the monster lived in our minds for only a short time before we released it into Starosibirsk, and then the world.

We carved claw marks into the trees with the knives from our kitchens. We used soup ladles and potato mashers to dig footprints into the soil. We dipped our fingers into varenye jam and smudged misshapen handprints onto shop windows. We trampled through bushes to create the monster's paths, roaring from the bottoms of our stomachs as we went. We collected long silver hairs from the babushki and scattered them everywhere—

onto the sides of buildings, where we imagined our monster would scratch itself when shedding in warm weather, and onto piles of dried leaves, beneath which we imagined our monster would sleep.

We wanted, too, for the monster to appear intelligent. So we carved furniture from larch wood scraps and placed it in clearings near the edge of the forest, in places villagers did not often go. Rocking chairs and tables, a grand bed with four twisted posts. Clumsy, unsophisticated things, but strange enough to provoke unease.

Then we captured the footage using borrowed camera equipment and posted it to the online message boards. Above each photograph and video, we wrote: Come See for Yourself the Dreadful and Specific Monster of Starosibirsk!

The story flowed easily, like water. We counted the responses. We watched the curiosity go up, up, up.

And when the tourists began to come, we were ready for them.

I am willing to admit—that is, you should know, if it is not obvious already—that I was not innocent in all of this. It would not have become what it was without the efforts of the Sighters. I was one of them: the appointed Sighter of Starosibirsk-Between-the-Bakery-and-the-Lightpost-That-Does-Not-Work. We divided the village into small, manageable parcels, and each Sighter had their own domain.

It was part of the tour experience we had agreed on. A guided tour felt too forced, not authentic. Instead, as visitors arrived, they were greeted by a series of hints: the footprints; two competing smells in the air, one like a wet dog, the other industrial, metallic. Next—and this was important—they encountered their first Sighter.

The Sighters entertained tourists with tales of our monster. We played the role of the believers, the ones who had seen. There was a Sighter of Starosibirsk-Between-the-Primary-School-and-the-Produce-Shop and another of Starosibirsk-Where-the-Hills-Flatten-to-Meet-the-Shore. Everything we said was based on a script we had written that long night-turned-to-morning in the tavern. Though we had a certain amount of freedom in telling the stories, we knew consistency was essential to the lie.

We took our jobs seriously. We rehearsed.

"I am a hunter," one Sighter would say, pointing to a footprint in the soil. "I have tracked animals all my life, and I know without a doubt this cannot be the mark of a bear."

"I am a mushroom picker," another would say, pointing to the stripped-away bark of a tree. "I have foraged fungi my whole life, and I know without a doubt they could not have caused this decay."

Or: "I am a carpenter. I have made furniture my whole life. No village in this region would produce something so rudimentary. Without a doubt, I know it to be the monster's nest."

And it worked just as we hoped it would. Slowly at first, mostly thrill seekers who appreciated this kind of thing more than most. Who had already seen all the monster movies. Who had already been buried alive at that novelty tourist attraction several days away from Starosibirsk on the Trans-Siberian Railway, the one that had been featured on the British travel show. These groups were eager to believe. They made it easy. They came to stalk, to kill.

Gradually, the village filled. The guesthouses were at least half-booked and the cafes felt warmer now that the ovens were on, browning meat pastries, while garlic-rich solyanka stew bubbled on the stove. Some visitors knew the history of Starosibirsk, knew of the exquisite saltiness of the sturgeon eggs and the breadth and stillness of the once-giving river. But others did not, and to them, we were a small village, not spectacular, one of many affected by the accident at the nickel factory, which appeared only briefly in the national news.

Now, we can look at our plan and see the errors. But we were too close to it then. We had already printed T-shirts with images of the monster, displayed them next to matching wood carvings in the abandoned building we had converted to a souvenir shop.

We did not look around us or above us—only at the coins that once again, thankfully, necessarily, found their way into our tills.

So when the chickens turned up dead, feathers bloody and necks mangled, set at odd angles and bitten through, and the tourists looked at one another with gleeful terror, we thought: wolves. Until one of Varvara's brothers took responsibility.

Yes, we were attracting enough tourists now, he said, but how long would it be until they lost interest? They were desensitized, skuchayushchiy, like all of us. They saw worse on their televisions every day. How long would false footprints and

claw marks on trees convince them?

And it made sense well enough. We applauded him for taking initiative. We toasted him at the tavern and piled on his plate all of our extra pickles and herring.

When the howls rang through the village and the tourists screamed in delight, we thought: a mother brown bear defending her young. But this time, it was the baker who took credit. He said when he watched the American movies, he was most fascinated by the sound effects.

When the sounds of claws scraping the outsides of buildings, too close to our pillows, woke us from our sleep, and the next morning we looked for an answer, the bartender's wife raised her hand with satisfaction.

When we felt hot breath on the backs of our necks, we did not even give it a second thought. We assumed it was one of us, practicing a stunt that would later be used on the tourists. We gave each other knowing looks. We stopped asking, supposed everything was of our own making.

It became a competition. A matter of pride. Even Yuri, the gentlest among us, spent long hours in the tavern's dark corners, inventing new ways to make our monster more terrifying than before.

Borya had been bragging about a big plan that would outdo all the rest. And we knew his family owned a herd of cattle. So when one tour group found the bony, spotted bodies lined up on the shore, flies buzzing, tongues hanging from mouths, we thought: okay, Borya, a little dramatic, but nice touch. The cows were clearly the sickest and weakest of the herd. Their eyes were half-lidded and their sides heaved from the effort of staying alive.

And as we played our foolish games, the stories traveled and the visitors came in greater numbers. They said they had heard the monster of Starosibirsk was *extreme*. When the guesthouses were full, we housed them in our own cottages, giving up our beds to them while we slept on spare blankets on splintered wood floors.

We were already overcrowded, already beyond capacity, when the famous interview aired and we completely lost control.

The interview was with an influential politician who had been criticized consistently for the brutality of his decisions, and the coldness and swiftness with which he made them. Probably you know it. Probably you watched it, more than once, and probably this is how you heard of

Starosibirsk in the first place. This particular interview had to do with the politician's involvement in the nickel and copper industries, and those industries' effects on the natural environment.

If you have seen the interview, you know what he said. In case you have not, I will repeat it:

"The people of this country have no gratitude. They call me a monster. But look at the good I have done—would you call this the work of a monster? You know, if you want a monster, go to the village of Starosibirsk. Do you know this place? Strashno! Go, and you will learn the meaning of the word."

We did not know how the politician had heard about us. But it was at this point that we knew we were doomed.

The politician was a controversial figure, and the interview was the most watched television broadcast that year. Within a week, the cars that had been coming to Starosibirsk were replaced by bright-colored multi-deck buses organized by travel agents in the western cities. Tourists came from farther and farther away. The buses had chains around their wheels and snowplows attached in front to ensure no number of traditional Siberian obstacles could stop them.

Remember: Once, Starosibirsk was all wet soil and sharp-grassed meadows, the smell of wood smoke rising from chimneys, empty spaces between A-frame structures, the occasional flutter of a floral apron when glorious Varvara came into the room. After the interview, it was packed tight with bodies. Bare arms in the summer months, and chalky sun cream, and perfumed sweat. Then in the winter, hats and boots and furs, and still that awful stench beneath those as the tourists flooded in.

We tried to keep up with the demand. The Sighters stayed true to our scripts, for the most part, shouting the fabrications louder and louder so the groups, larger and larger, could hear them. Some listened intently, others half-listened, others not at all, instead peering around for signs of the local monster.

The bartender expanded the tavern into the building across the street. The bakery opened earlier and closed later, and the baker hired more of his cousins to work shifts producing the farmer's-cheese vatrushka, a popular snack among the tourists, who liked to eat it as they walked, exploring the village, looking for blood.

Then, hell.

Dima's loyal mutt, the undersized borzoi, was found gutted at the edge of the water, his ribs cracked open and the cavity filled with maggots and opportunistic birds.

The tourist who found the borzoi wore heeled boots into the forest and took a disposable camera roll's worth of photographs of the scene. She shook with excitement. She said she felt lucky to have had such an *authentic* experience, to be the one among her friends to uncover another piece of the mystery that day.

Dima was in ruins.

We called a meeting.

More and more, our horrific acts had convinced the tourists of the monster's existence. More and more, we were unconvinced that we had done the right thing.

At the tavern, closed off to tourists that night only, we questioned everyone: If Borya had killed the cattle, what would stop him from taking the next step? Or Varvara's brother, with the chickens, could he have gone too far? Or Mikhail, who had put this whole wretched idea on the table and then left it there, like so many fish, to rot?

Who showed the most hunger for the money the new tourism had brought us? Who was the most competitive? Who had the most to lose, to gain? The air between us was thick with distrust and every person, declining Yuri's offers, would consume only the drinks they poured themselves.

Then the confessions came, spilling faster than vodka.

"The chickens. I lied," said Varvara's brother.

"The scraping noises. I lied," added the bartender's wife.

"The cattle. I lied," admitted Borya finally, dropping his head to his chest. Refusing to meet Dima's eyes.

We had been so willing to take ownership when we thought the only thing we were stealing was credit from some bashful party. But Dima's eyes, the empty bottle before him. This could never have been part of our game.

You know the rest, it is safe to say. The deep scratches in the paint of the multi-deck buses. The missing tourists and the parts of them that, eventually, we recovered. An ear, a finger, a heeled boot, the manicured foot still inside. The missing villagers, too.

And a small village on a wide, calm river that, despite it all, remains overrun. The more mutilated bodies appear swollen in the water or bent around the branches of trees, the more living, sweating bodies appear at the train station—always in high spirits, ready to hunt. Yes, they have even reopened the station. In fact, Starosibirsk is the busiest stop on the eastbound line. Everyone is a suspect, and the number of suspects grows each day.

As for us, we again take a scientific approach.

Our observation: Fiction is believable. The truth is not. We have all done terrible things, sought them out for amusement, been ignorant and short-sighted when thinking about our own survival.

Our question: Who is responsible for the deaths? Man or monster? One of us, or one of them, or something else entirely?

Our hypothesis:

This is where I come in. I am still Arseny, the Sighter of Starosibirsk-Between-the-Bakery-and-the-Lightpost-That-Does-Not-Work; at least when the tourists are out, during the day. The rest of the time, I have appointed myself Arseny the detective. There is a task force. The original six, the ones who started it all.

We work furiously in the tavern, drawing timelines and circling, then crossing out, names. We think fondly of the uncommon sturgeon and the warning songs we learned as children, when we still saw a clear line between what was wrong and right, a line moving in one direction between the eaters and the eaten.

We circle names. We cross them out. Yuri distributes the vodka. Dima raps his knuckles against the table but is otherwise silent.

Something howls in the near distance.

We huddle together, praying we can find again some logic in this world.

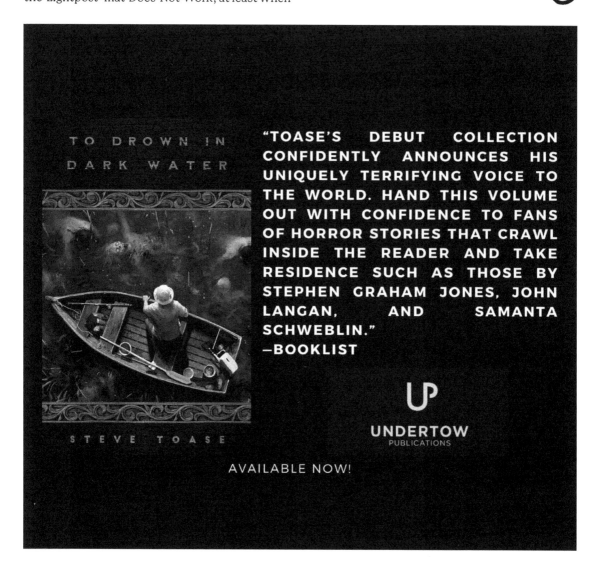

THE OUTER DARK
PODCAST & SYMPOSIUM

Our mission is to foster conversation and connect communities among the diverse slate of creators and audience members under the umbrella of speculative fiction - inclusive, safe and welcoming to women, LBGTQIA+, and writers of color.

LISTEN ON THIS IS HORROR   TWITTER @THEOUTERDARK   THEOUTERDARK.ORG

THE
MACABRE
READER

BOOK REVIEWS BY LYSETTE STEVENSON

BEHOLD THE UNDEAD OF DRACULA: LURID TALES OF CINEMATIC GOTHIC HORROR
edited by Jonathan Raab of Muzzleland Press. Cover by Toronto artist Trevor Henderson. 2019

This mouldering crypt of eleven coffins opens with the pandemonium of Matthew M. Bartlett followed closely behind in wraithlike grace by Gwendolyn Kiste and closing with the indomitable Gemma Files in a multi-narrative love letter to the late 50's through early 70's heyday of Hammer Horror productions.

Embracing Hammer's signature style of sex, violence and technicolour gore, this collection celebrates perpetual autumn and the melodramatic atmosphere of the fog shrouded moors. Where monsters hunker in bat infested castles as torch lit paths through the forest lead to shadowed villages. While other stories take you into the film studios and behind the scenes, where lead actors meet their grim demise and gothic heroines twist the narrative of their fate.

Each story is also capped with author notes allowing the reader an intimate look into the writers' creative process as they reflect on their personal experiences with Hammer's gothic films. Common themes of early exposure to the creature features on late night television or the, now collectable, movie tie-in books. Seeing Basil Gogos' illustration of Christopher Lee on the cover of *Famous Monsters of Filmland*, to being a goth girl or a middle-American youth finding kinship in British folk horror. An iconic and beloved era of cinema, this anthology is a playful homage to that lustful enthusiasm for the macabre and all things that creak and shriek in the night.

COME TOMORROW AND OTHER TALES OF BANGALORE TERROR
by Jayaprakash Satyamurthy. Published in India by Notion Press, 2020. Cover by Bangalore illustrator Anoop Bhat.

Writer and musician Jayaprakash Satyamurthy's collection of spectral horrors contain overlapping timelines and characters that take you through the haunted thresholds and portals of his hometown Bangalore. The most tech driven city in southern India, Satyamurthy explores what happens to the ghosts of slums that are raised and gentrified, or when five star hotels are erected over the abandoned temples of gods. To glimpses into the Indian metal scene where a guitar player delves perilously into the occult and an initiatory gathering at an arcane lodge pushes the boundaries of the members' sanity.

The attention to pacing and rhythmic language draws you into each of these stories, whether they lean to folk or corporate horror narratives. The weird slips into each protagonist's life in ways as unsettling as they are captivating.

Many of the stories in *Come Tomorrow* were originally published in two chapbooks; *Weird Tales of a Bangalorean* and *A Volume of Sleep,* both of which are still available in North America. This re-release was primarily to make Satyamurthy's work available for the English market in India. Jayaprakash additionally writes music and plays bass guitar in doom metal band Djinn & Miskatonic. He also has a 2020 collection of poetry out called *Broken Cup* published by Clash Books.

FLESH & BLOOD: A HISTORY OF THE CANNIBAL COMPLEX
by Reay Tannahill. Published in the UK by Hamish Hamilton, 1975.

In researching her first book on *The History of Food,* Scottish

historian Reay Tannahill said she encountered so many accounts of cannibalism across centuries and cultures, that she felt she had a book's worth on the subject. Her blackened sense of humor moves throughout this extensively annotated work. She explores the origins of cannibalism from population control and famine induced survival. The folklore that gave us vampires, werewolves, witches and ghouls, to religious devotions and acts of war. Reading the plethora of documentation the mind gradually acclimatizes to the last great taboo. From the chilling account of a doctor living in Cairo during the Egypt famine of 1201, Abd al-Latif records dispassionately the vast extent of death and subsequent feasting happening openly in the streets. Tannahill takes the reader through history to see how widespread the practice of graverobbing was or how often the burned bodies of witch trials were scavenged for dinner. In depth looks at the savagery of Lady Bathory and the perversity of the Butcher of Hanover. One begins to understand cultural rituals in South America, honor and revenge from the Norse to the Polynesians or the basic will to live when stranded on a mountain or at sea. Closing the book the true horror is that any one of us are capable given the circumstances and the perpetrators of cannibalism frequently recall that at first they absolutely refused to eat the flesh of another but once they partook, they began to crave it. Fittingly Tannahill's follow up book was on *The History of Sex.*

PHANTASM/CHIMERA: AN ANTHOLOGY OF STRANGE AND TROUBLING DREAMS,
2017 edited by Scott Dwyer of Plutonian Press. Cover by Ukrainian artist Serhiy Krykun.

Nightmares take us through territory off kilter, familiar yet strange and into worlds unknown. They are a mediation between realms where we are neither living nor dead. Inspired by the dark surrealism of Kafka and the highly stylized gore of Italian filmmaker Lucio Fulci; anthologist Scott Dwyer, sought to curate a collection outside of the horror mainstream for readers like himself, who not only want to see beyond the gates of hell but also want to be ravished by it. Eleven stories ranging broadly from the unsettling and bizarre to bleak and pessimistic and the ghoulishly carnal, characters grapple with nightmare logic invading their mundane lives. From a phantasmagorical children's birthday party to backwoods drug dealers. Folklore studies in the Japanese diaspora and parasitic alien lifeforms, to a loveless marriage unhinged by animal ciphers or the sonic booms of a vexed sorceress. When the alluring turns vile, haunted by shadows and things that cannot be verified nor unseen no matter how hard we resist, the rational world must be left behind. While playing with the pantheon of nightmare horror, the writers of *Phantasm/Chimera* invite you into the outer world; the sinuous charnel house of dreams. Upstate New York based micropress Plutonian, curates invite only anthologies of new work by exemplary writers within and on the fringe of the weird horror field. In 2019, Plutonian released its second anthology this time exploring the theme of horror and the erotic titled: *Pluto in Furs.*

PLAYGHOUL MAGAZINE: SPECIAL VAMPIRA ISSUE!
2019, compiled by the mysterious Mighty Moloch of Coney Islands' Phantom Creep Theatre. Cover art by Donald David.

Through the feverish collecting of pulp magazines and newspaper articles circa 1950 to 1964, *Playghoul* is the most exhumed archive of the Vampira oeuvre in print. Finnish-American, Maila Nurmi was a burgeoning artist, stage actress, model and dancer in 1940's Los Angeles when she crafted the character of Vampira inspired by Charles Addams Morticia. The original Scream Queen horror host, The Vampira Show was a short lived horror movie segment on syndicated television spawning nation wide fan clubs and tabloid gossip involving her relationship with the doomed James Dean.

Playing up the camp with her voluptuous black widow figure she was the first celebrated glamour ghoul and an early pioneer of goth and punk fashion. Asked about the popularity of her creation Malia answered "People have so much repressed evil they need a character to identify with."

Playghoul Magazine was bound by hand at almost half an inch thick and beautifully reproduced with offset-screen printing. Contemporary advertising that helped spirit this DIY production into existence blends with the 50's era aesthetics. A midstream Phantom Creep Theatre comic series recreates the midnight movies Vampira would have been introducing on her show.

The initial print run of 666 paperbacks proved so popular it quickly sold out. It has since been re-released as a deluxe edition hardcover with a potential second volume of Vampira's later years in the works.

THE BLIND OWL
by Sadegh Hedayat published by Grove Press, 1957. Translated from Persian by D. P. Costello.

Since its first publication in 1936, *The Blind Owl* has been widely translated and republished throughout the world. In Iran, superstition still circulates that it is alleged to have induced a spate of suicides and Iranian youth are dissuaded from reading it.

This nightmarish journey chronicles an unnamed narrator's confessions to an owl shaped shadow on the wall of his claustrophobic dwelling. He desires to love and to truly live before he dies but is consumed by omens of death all around him. In a dream-like haze of alcohol and opium the labyrinthine narration re-encounters the same cast of characters. Whether peering out his window at skeletal black horses pulling a hearse past the butcher shop, or artistically rendered on the pen cases he paints, to visions of the lost land of Rey. Through the dissociated fragments of the narrator's psyche the reader is drawn into the mystery and its horrific discoveries. Eloquent and lyrical, with at times an acerbic wit, it is a true descent into isolation and madness, where moments of tenderness and reprieve are found amongst the dead.

Lauded as the Persian Poe, Sadegh Hedayat was born into an aristocratic Tehranian family. He lived as a writer and translator, where among his works was translating Franz Kafka into Farsi, in mid-century Paris, where he tragically ended his life.

TORTURE GARDEN
by Octave Mirbeau first published 1899 in French. Translated, unabridged 1965, Lancer paperback with introduction by L.T. Woodward, M.D. Cover art by Frank Frazetta.

Paris 1899, amidst the upheaval of the Dreyfus Affair and

the artistic and literary movements of the fin-de-siecle; author, anarchist and champion of the avant-garde Octave Mirbeau penned a novel that pushed all boundaries of transgression and morality, baring the hypocrisies of French society.

Opening with a drawing room discussion on the nature of mankind and his inherent lust for violence, a man seemingly drained of life recounts his past debaucheries and the woman who showed him a world of far richer depravities. The unnamed narrator, as part of a political cover up, takes a journey to the far east where he falls in love with a woman for her perceived virtue and beauty. This sardonic love story climaxes in an exotic tropical garden engulfed within a Cantonese prison complex. Here patrons of torture witness and engage in prolonged acts of cruelty and suffering. Creating a symbiosis of blood, flesh and bone to feed and fertilize the garden of extraordinary flora and fauna.

Mirbeau satirizes the corrosion of French politics and a Western society that readily wears masks of virtuousness. Where repression and opulence breed immorality and sadism for the punishment of petty crimes. At the turn of the century as humanity transcends, everything pales before the *Torture Garden*. One hundred and twenty years later this book is still capable of shocking even the most jaded horror fans amongst us.

WITCHES STILL LIVE: A STUDY OF THE BLACK ART TODAY

by Theda Kenyon. Published 1929 by Ives Washburn, with sublime woodcut illustrations by artist William Siegel.

Theda Kenyon approaches this material keenly as a researcher with a naturally engaging narrative style. Drawing from sources as varied as Michelet's *La Sorciere* and Leland's *Aradia: Gospel of Witches,* to the *Occult Review* and the *New York Times*. She makes a compelling case that The Cult of the Witch is as universally ancient as it is relevant today. Beginning with records of early lore and doctrine, to descriptions of the Black Mass, sacrifice and sex-ritual to folk magic and widespread persecution. 'Witchcraft: The Universal Faith' as she calls it, is vividly brought to life. While there are reproductions available, in my opinion, the 100 year old mustiness and thick rough-edged paper, string lash binding and block print art makes finding an original edition a near fetish.

In 2018 my brother and father were called to a remote cabin by the widow of a man who had filled it to the ceiling with an impressive library of esoterica. If it wasn't for the dozen feral cats who roamed the cabin freely and sprayed the library extensively they would have simply bought the whole collection. Over the course of a week they scoured the shelves through what was an impenetrable stench and salvaged what they could. Thankfully, Witches Still Live was among pristine books on a top shelf. What couldn't be saved of the library was piled outside of the cabin and burned.

ABBERANT VISIONS

FILM REVIEWS BY TOM GOLDSTEIN

BECKY (2020)
Starring: Lulu Wilson, Kevin James, Robert Maillet, et al.
Directors: Jonathan Milott, Cary Murnion
Writers: Nick Morris, Ruckus Skye
Running Time: 100 minutes

A group of escaped convicts get more than they bargain for when they mess with Becky, a grieving teen who—in the words of one character—is "determined and as vindictive as they come."

The movie is like an out-door version of *Home Alone*, although Lulu Wilson's title character is not as adorable as Macaulay Culkin's Kevin McCallister. She seems to have taken a survivalist militia training course, as well as one in one-sided transactionalism from Donald Trump.

A bloody and somewhat breezy affair.

A GOOD WOMAN IS HARD TO FIND (2019)
Starring: Sarah Bolger, Edward Hogg, Andrew Simpson, et.al.
Director: Abner Pastoll
Writer: Ronan Blaney
Running time: 97 minutes

ISOLANI (2017)
Starring: Kate McLaughlin, Catriona Evans, Jim Sweeney, Gianni Capaldi, et. al.
Director: R. Paul Wilson
Writer: R. Paul Wilson
Running time: 110 minutes.

Two British films about young single moms trying to protect their kids in the aftermath of murder. Two different approaches.

A Good Woman is Hard to Find is a splatterfest (you'll get that right off the top) black comedy. The mom here is treated like a doormat by the various men who enter her life as she tries to find out who

murdered her husband. Once she's pushed too far, the blood begins to spew. Fans of the genre will probably like it, but it's basically been-there, done that, although not always with the same panache as *A Good Woman...*

Isolani, on the other hand, is a thought-provoking slow-burn. It deals with moral issues that concern the crossing of lines: How much are you willing to tolerate before you say No? How much are you willing to accept from someone very close to you before their actions become unforgivable? Well written and well-acted, *Isolani* is well worth viewing.

TIGERS ARE NOT AFRAID (2017)
Starring: Paola Lara, Juan Ramon Lopez, Nery Arredondo, et. al.
Director: Issa Lopez
Writer: Issa Lopez
Running Time: 83 minutes

Orphaned street kids form a family of sorts to survive amid the terror and horror of Mexico's ultra-violent

Becky (2020)

drug wars. Reminiscent of the early work of Guillermo del Toro, this dark fairy tale is haunting, terrifying and beautiful. BTW, del Toro and Tigers director/writer Issa Lopez are reportedly collaborating on a werewolf Western.

DEAD DICKS (2019)
Starring: Heston Horwin, Jillian Harris, Matt Keyes, et. al.
Directors: Chris Bavota, Lee Paula Springer
Writers: Chris Bavota, Lee Paula Springer
Running time: 83 minutes

This is not a film about detectives or erectile dysfunction. The story centres on a guy named Richie, which like Dick, is a diminutive for Richard. Richie keeps trying to kill himself—and is successful. The thing is he won't stay dead. So he keeps trying, and trying. As a result, his apartment is strewn with his corpses: laying in the bathtub, hanging from the ceiling, etc.

Obviously this dark Canadian riff on Groundhog Day with its themes of mental illness and suicide is not for everyone. But it's surprisingly sweet at times and those with a twisted sense of humour should get a laugh out of it.

THE HUNT (2020)
Starring: Betty Gilpin, Hillary Swank, et. al.
Director: Craig Zobel
Writers: Nick Cuse, Damon Lindelof
Running time: 90 minutes

A group of good ol' boys and gals wake up in a clearing, not knowing where they are or how they got there. In various groups, they hit the road and encounter locals whose smiling faces—as the song says—tell lies. Turns out these "deplorables" are the sport in a game played by "libtards." Over-all, it's not a bad satire of current U.S. political culture. It's best, however, near the end when it takes aim at social media, showing what can happen when you take on the wrong—in more ways than one—person.

FATMAN (2020)
Starring: Mel Gibson, Walton Goggins, Marianne Jean-Baptiste, et. al
Directors: Eshom Nelms, Ian Nelms
Writers: Ian Nelms, Eshom Nelms
Running time: 100 minutes

After receiving a lump of coal for Christmas an obnoxious, bratty rich kid hires a hitman to kill Santa, or Chris Cringle as he goes by in this film which is more Bad-ass Santa than Bad Santa.

But milk and cookies aside, Chris is no softie. "You think I got this job 'cuz I'm fat and jolly?" he scowls at one point. And he has rolodexes and reams of files to keep track of whose been naughty and nice, which he uses to lay on the emotional hurt while willing to mix it up physically.

Fatman is more Christmas jeer than Christmas cheer, but it's not a total lump of coal, thanks in part to the motherly influence of Mrs. Cringle.

Dead Dicks (2019)

ONE CUT OF THE DEAD
(KAMERA WO TOMERUNA!)
(2017)
Starring: Takayuki Hamatsu,
Yuzuki Akiyama, Harumi
Shuhama, et. al.
Director: Shin'ichiro Ueda
Writer: Shin'ichiro Ueda
(screenplay), Ryoichi Wada
(play)
Running time: 96 minutes

DEERSKIN (2019)
Starring: Jean Dujardin, Adele
Haenel
Director: Quentin Dupieux
Writer: Quentin Dupieux
Running time: 77 minutes

Two foreign films involving
filmmaking.

The first half-hour of Japan's
One Cut of the Dead is a
no-budget zombie flick that's
pretty generic.

The balance of the movie is a
flashback "making of." And it's
what makes the whole enter-
prise special. It's an homage to
independent film-making—the
creative process, the innovation
and the blood, sweat and tears
to get it done.

France's *Deerskin*, on the
other hand, is another example
of European WTF horror. It's
about a middle age guy who,
after an acrimonious divorce,
drives into the French country-
side to buy the deerskin jacket
he's coveted. The seller throws
in a digital movie camera as a

bonus. Our hero then decides
to pass himself off as a filmmaker, talking people into loan-
ing him their jackets, which he
promptly purloins. That's so he
can pursue his quest to become
the only person in the world
with a jacket—don't ask. He's
egged on in his pursuit by his
newly acquired deerskin, which
talks—sort of. He also hooks
up with a barmaid who just
happens to be an an unem-
ployed film editor, who looks
at his raw footage, says she
gets his his vision, but tells him
the film needs more action. He
provides that with the help of a
sharpened blade from a ceiling
fan—it doesn't talk.

What we have is a weird-
ed-out tale of dealing with
midlife trauma. The actors
are acclaimed: Jean Dujardin won best actor award for
The Artist and Adele Haenel
starred in *A Portrait of a Lady
on Fire*, which won a couple
of awards at the 2019 Cannes
Film Festival. As for writer/

director Quentin Dupieux, he
was behind the cult favourite,
Rubber, the story of a discarded
tire that goes on a killing roll.

SPONTANEOUS (2020)
Starring: Katherine Langford,
Charlie Plummer, Yvonne Orj,
et.al.
Director: Brian Duffield
Writers: Brian Duffield (adapta-
tion), Aaron Starmer (novel)
Running time: 101 minutes

High school students blow up
(blood 'n' guts style) randomly
and for no apparent reason in
this adaptation of a young adult
novel.

Amid the helplessness and
senselessness, relationships
form and evolve and the lead
character acquires a wisdom
that so many of us could use in
this bizarre real-life
era we're stuck in.

A fun time for a
difficult time.

Spontaneous (2020)

Art by Grandfailure

DIM SHORES is a micropress publisher of weird fictions in various flavors, including cosmic horror, dark fantasy, surreal science fiction, and the unclassifiably strange. Most publications are limited-edition chapbooks, lovingly hand-numbered and packed with care at Dim Shores headquarters in California.

A new anthology and at least two chapbooks are coming in 2021. For more information or to be added to the mailing list, visit dimshores.com.

DIM SHORES

POST OFFICE BOX 3092
CITRUS HEIGHTS, CA
95611-3092, USA
DIMSHORES.COM

CONTRIBUTORS

MARIA ABRAMS is a graphic designer and professor who lives in Colorado. When not trying to scare people, she enjoys staying active and making stuff. Find her at www.abramstheauthor.com.

MARY BERMAN is a Philadelphia-based writer of science fiction, fantasy, and horror. She earned her MFA in fiction from the University of Mississippi, and her work has been published in *Fireside, Cicada, Daily Science Fiction,* and elsewhere. In her spare time, she takes fitness classes and antagonizes her cat. Find her online at www.mtgberman.com.

SAM COWAN is a layout and production artist based in Sacramento, CA. His nanopress Dim Shores publishes anthologies and chapbooks of weird fiction.

WESLEY EDWARDS is a freelance artist living in Dallas, TX, he works for a variety of independent publications and sells commissions and prints through his website at www.wesleyedwardsart.com. You can also find his work on Instagram, Facebook and Twitter @wesleyedwardsart.

ROB FRANCIS is an academic and writer based in London. He mainly writes short fantasy and horror, and his stories have appeared in magazines such as *The Arcanist, Apparition Lit, Metaphorosis, Tales to Terrify* and *Novel Noctule*. Rob has also contributed stories to several anthologies, including *DeadSteam* by Grimmer & Grimmer books, *Under the Full Moon's Light* by Owl Hollow Press, and *Scare Me* by Esskaye Books. He is an affiliate member of the HWA. Rob lurks on Twitter @RAFurbaneco

TOM GOLDSTEIN spent about 35 years working in various capacities in newsrooms of major newspapers across Canada — as a reporter, editor and a couple of extracurricular stints as a music or video reviewer. He has never — and still does not — consider himself a critic. Rather he's just a guy who really likes movies, with a particular interest in "different."

ORRIN GREY is a skeleton who likes monsters as well as the author of several spooky books. His stories of ghosts, monsters, and sometimes the ghosts of monsters can be found in dozens of anthologies, including Ellen Datlow's *Best Horror of the Year*. He resides in the suburbs of Kansas City and watches lots of scary movies. You can visit him online at orringrey.com.

NICK GUCKER is an illustrator and painter of the weird, horrific and unusual. He resides in the damp mist enshrouded climes of Seattle, WA. When not preoccupied with kaiju toys and harvesting mushrooms from behind his ears. He and his wife Denise engage in frequent imaginary kung fu kitchen battles and marathon cat belly rubbing sessions. To learn more about his art and his familiars, visit Nick at nickthehatart.com.

VINCE HAIG is an illustrator, designer, and author. You can visit Vince at his website: barquing.com

MARC JOAN is a biomedical scientist and inventor of stories. He was raised in India—a seminal experience which informs much of his writing. He has published ~25 stories and one novelette ('The Speckled God', Unsung Stories, 2017), and is finalising two novels and three collections of short stories. Competition results include: Aesthetica Creative Writing Award 2017/2018 (finalist); Ink Tears Short Story

Competition 2017/18 (runner up); Galley Beggar Short Story Competition 2017/18 (special mention); Brighton Prize 2017 (long-listed); 2018 BBC National Short Story Award (last 60 from ~1,000 entries); CRAFT Short Fiction Prize 2020 (top 4%); Punt Volat / Spencer Parker Memorial Award 2020 (winner); 2020 William van Dyke Short Story Prize (long-listed); and 2020 Gatehouse Press New Fiction Award (Highly Commended). www.marc-joan.com https://www.facebook.com/marc.joan.35/

ALYS KEY is a British writer and journalist living in East London. In 2019 she won the Benjamin Franklin House Literary Prize. This is her first published fiction in a magazine.

Nova Scotian writer **CATHERINE MACLEOD** loves chai tea, television soundtracks, and overheard conversations. Her publications include short fiction in *Nightmare, Black Static, On Spec, Tor.com,* and several anthologies, including *Fearful Symmetries* and *Playground of Lost Toys.* Her story "Hide and Seek" won the inaugural Sunburst Award for Short Story.

EVAN JAMES SHELDON's work has appeared recently in the *American Literary Review,* the *Cincinnati Review,* and the *Maine Review,* among other journals. He is a Senior Editor for *F(r)iction* and the Editorial Director for Brink Literacy Project. You can find online at evanjamessheldon.com.

LYSETTE STEVENSON is a stage manager with a rural outdoor equestrian theatre company and a second generation bookseller. She lives in British Columbia.

SIMON STRANTZAS is the author of five collections of short fiction, including *Nothing is Everything* (Undertow Publications, 2018), and editor of a number of anthologies, including *Year's Best Weird Fiction, Vol. 3.* Combined, he's been a finalist for four Shirley Jackson Awards, two British Fantasy Awards, and the World Fantasy Award. His fiction has appeared in numerous annual best-of anthologies, and in venues such as *Nightmare, The Dark,* and *Cemetery Dance.* In 2014, his edited anthology, *Aickman's Heirs,* won the Shirley Jackson Award. He lives with his wife in Toronto, Canada.

KRISTINA TEN is a Russian-American writer of short fiction and poetry with work in *Lightspeed, Black Static, AE Science Fiction,* and elsewhere. She is a 2019 graduate of Clarion West Writers Workshop and a current MFA candidate at the University of Colorado Boulder. You can find her at kristinaten.com and on Twitter as @kristina_ten.

STEPHEN VOLK is best known as writer of the BBC's notorious "Halloween hoax" *Ghostwatch* and the ITV paranormal drama series *Afterlife.* His other screenplays include *The Awakening* (2011), *Midwinter of the Spirit* (2015), and *Gothic* starring Natasha Richardson as Mary Shelley. He is a BAFTA winner, two-time British Fantasy Award winner, and the author of three collections: *Dark Corners, Monsters in the Heart,* and *The Parts We Play,* while *The Dark Masters Trilogy* consists of stories featuring Peter Cushing, Alfred Hitchcock and Dennis Wheatley respectively. His astringent non-fiction is collected in *Coffinmaker's Blues: Collected Writings on Terror.* www.stephenvolk.net.

9 781988 964300